About the Author

Lynda Florence Hughes is retired, and lives in a market town in Dorset about ten miles from the ocean. She is the proud mother of two sons and a grandson. Lynda has spent a lot of time in the Far East, travelling, making new friends and embracing new cultures. This is where she re-discovered her love of writing. One of her stories was shortlisted for a literary prize. This is her debut novel.

Losing the Thread

Lynda Florence Hughes

Losing the Thread

Olympia Publishers
London

www.olympiapublishers.com
OLYMPIA PAPERBACK EDITION

A CIP catalogue record for this title is
available from the British Library.

ISBN: 978-1-80074-798-2

This is a work of fiction.
Names, characters, places and incidents originate from the writer's
imagination. Any resemblance to actual persons, living or dead, is
purely coincidental.

First Published in 2023

Olympia Publishers
Tallis House
2 Tallis Street
London
EC4Y 0AB

Printed in Great Britain

Dedication

I would like to dedicate my debut novel to the memory of my wonderful parents; Florence and Ernest, and my dear brother, Leslie Duncan Nuttall.

Acknowledgements

I should like to convey my warmest thanks to everyone who helped to bring this book from pip to blossom. All who have encouraged, listened, chuckled and believed, especially Mary Bé, who helped with some early pruning and shaping, then supported me throughout the whole process. My beloved Daniel, Ben and Gemma, and all my other treasured family members, thanks for your faith in me. I'm grateful to my fabulous "Penn Hill book club girls" for their enthusiasm and laughter. All my friends have played their part, but special thanks go to RJ, Caz and the two Pams, who buoyed me up when the going got tough. I'd like to show gratitude to the team at Olympia Publishing. Between them they helped to entice out the final shiny fruit. And lastly, I want to thank Jamil, my mentor and friend. Without him the pip would never even have got planted. His gifts to me are beyond words

Sat Chit Ananda

CHAPTER ONE

The day it all began was unremarkable. There was no indication of what was to follow, and neither of the two women, on that crisp sunny autumnal morning, realised just how much their lives would change.

Paula drove on to the forecourt of the transformed premises, excited to hear the crunch of tyres on newly laid shingle. She walked purposefully towards the large oak door, inserted her key and stepped inside. Clearing her brain of random thoughts, she tapped the alarm system keypad with confidence.

Walking into the converted barn, she looked around with pride, thrilled with the prospect of what lay ahead in the inspiring new location of Gingham and Velvet.

Paula and Nicky, her business partner, had similar taste, therefore choosing the layout, decor and furnishings had been relatively easy and enjoyable in the main. Over time they came to understand that subtraction creates more beauty than addition. The art of realising what is essential, and giving it ample space, was found to be far more effective than trying to cram in too much. This trick had to be learnt by the two women, mind you. Challenging decisions had to be made from time to time. They had been assisted with the design and blueprint of the barn by a rather exacting architect. It had taken numerous meetings, lunches and the occasional dinner, for the three of them to agree on the final layout, which was then passed on to the town planners. After several months of frustrating hold-ups, the architectural plans were finally approved, and the conversion started to take shape.

The results were all around them every day.

The two women had come a long way since their humble beginnings, starting up their business from a large shed at the bottom of Nicky's garden. They were full of enthusiasm from the outset, both bursting with creative ideas, yet unsure how to turn their vision into a reality. There were times when, working into the night to complete an order, both bone tired and despondent, they could have caved in and given up on their dream.

It certainly hadn't all been plain sailing. There'd been many sleepless nights for the pair in the first few years, and very little cash. It had taken courage and determination from them both to continue to make a go of it. In the end though it was the passion they both felt for fabrics, textiles and design which sustained them through those testing times.

They had fallen into their roles quite naturally, Nicky being the real genius on a sewing machine. Paula enjoyed the creative part in the early stages of a bespoke original garment, but lost patience, and was cack-handed when it came down to the actual sewing. They had equal input into the designing process. Then Paula concentrated on the marketing and administration, whilst Nicky carried out the role of the seamstress, with her exquisite skills. They would collaborate, and discuss ideas, allowing for a healthy variation of opinion, but were careful not to give harmful critique. They felt strongly that doing so may stop creativity.

Whatever their method, it seemed to work.

Paula heard the front door slam, followed by a flurry of activity and a few choice cusses, as Nicky appeared, looking red, flustered and out of sorts.

'I can't believe it. I had them when I set off, I swear,' she complained, rummaging in her large bag. 'It's that re-cycled sack of remnants I was going to use for the Lambert job.'

'Calm down, Nicky,' laughed Paula. 'It's not the end of the world. There's plenty to be getting on with. You'll just have to leave the embellishing till tomorrow.'

'Hang on. I remember now, they're on the hall table by the door. I put them there so I wouldn't forget them. Honestly! Boy, that coffee smells good. I'm glad I persuaded you we needed that machine. I told you it was an essential, and not a luxury,' she teased.

Paula turned to give Nicky a rueful look, but couldn't help altering it into a grin. She had to concede her partner had been right all along about the decision to buy the fancy coffee machine, as well as the microwave which was also proving useful.

After pouring the steaming liquid into their two preferred mugs, she handed one to Nicky, and the two partners sat facing each other at the cream table in the bijou kitchen.

Nicky was dressed in her favourite outfit of dungarees, which, today, were pale blue light denim, underneath which was a bold, chequered fleecy shirt in reds and yellows. One of the broad straps had fallen off her shoulder, and she was trying to tighten the fastening with one hand, whilst attempting to drink her coffee with the other.

'Darn this thing,' she said, admitting defeat, putting down her French mug, and adjusting herself. Smiling broadly she took a long swig of the good strong brew and proceeded to fill Paula in on what she'd been doing over the weekend.

The telephone rang piercingly, startling the two women momentarily. Paula walked over to her desk to answer it.

'Gingham and Velvet,' she announced, in her business voice, 'how can I help you?'

Paula was taken aback when she heard the intonation at the other end of the line.

'This is Lady Phillipa Soames speaking,' announced her caller, in a loud upper-crust voice.

'Good morning, Lady Soames. This is Paulette Fredericks. What can I do for you today, Your Ladyship?' she asked pleasantly, with a quick wink to Nicky.

'I have been recommended to you by Dr Antony Vickers. I have an assignment I wish to discuss with you and your partner, requiring urgent attention,' she went on, hardly pausing for breath. 'I need to meet with you at your earliest convenience, to put together an extensive collection for my forthcoming winter cruise,' she finished, in a rush. 'I do need to emphasise the importance of being able to meet my precise standards, and to assure me you will work with maximum speed.'

Paula, who was a little taken aback at the exigency at which her prospective client was speaking, replied slowly and steadily, 'I shall consult our diaries, Lady Soames, and telephone you shortly to arrange a meeting. Would you like us to visit you at your home, or would you prefer to come to our business premises?'

'I must stress, that time is of the essence, Mrs Fredericks. Yes, I would prefer a home appointment. I will be at my country residence this coming week, which is close to you, as I'm led to believe we live in neighbouring counties. My country estate is in Hampshire. I will inform you of my address and directions when you decide to return my call,' she concluded, with a touch of derision.

'Very well, Lady Soames, I shall telephone you before the end of the day. I have your number displayed on my handset screen, thank you,' finished Paula carefully.

Paula replaced the hand set very deliberately.

'What was that all about, Mrs F? You look as mad as a hatter.'

'Of all the trumped up, rude, obnoxious... oooh... That was Lady Phillipa Soames. She is our potential new, self-important client. We are commanded to grace her with our presence urgently, apparently. We can't say no, Nicky, because, guess what, she wants a whole collection of outfits to take on her forthcoming winter cruise, no less. This could be a fantastic order for Gingham and Velvet, one of our biggest yet, it's just a shame she didn't sound more approachable. A Dr Antony Vickers recommended her. Do you know who that is?'

Nicky looked thoughtful, trying to remember where she'd heard the name before, but was unable to recall it immediately.

'It kind of rings a bell, but for the life of me, I don't know where from,' replied Nicky.

'Anyway, never mind about that, what a request. Get the diary out, let's sort out a date. We'd better not keep the 'lady' waiting,' warned Paula, pulling the diary towards her, and scanning the pages. After a cursory glance, she made a snap decision and went on.

'Thursday looks good to me. Nicky, you'd better zoom

home to collect that fabric after all, and get on with the Lambert order. I have a feeling it could be another late one, if we want to be clear by Thursday. I'll call Her Ladyship back and run through the usual questions. It's the same old, same old. They always leave it till the last minute to contact us, and of course, it's always urgent. Oh, by the way, could you pick up something tasty on your way back, please? I'm ravenous, and will collapse, frankly, if I don't eat,' said Paula in a faux dramatic tone.

'What happened to this week's diet, Paula?' teased Nicky.

Paula loved her food. She had a voluptuous, curvy, well-toned body, which she dressed largely in bohemian style clothes with quirky accessories. Her eye for colour, panache and flair were legendary. She could also rock the glamorous look when she felt the need. Her striking pale golden eyes resembled those of a lioness. Along with her olive skin and shiny straight mane of chestnut hair which just touched her shoulders, she genuinely had no idea what a captivating woman she was.

Nicky got up to make a quick exit, before Paula reacted to her taunt. Even though she would know it was a joke, Paula could get a little over sensitive when it came to weight issues.

'Go on with you, woman,' she shouted good-naturedly. 'You know I work better on a full tum!'

As Nicky left the building, she heard the phone buzzing again, but didn't stop to see who it was, eager to get on with the day's many challenges.

The phone continued to ring, and Paula sighed when she picked up, and heard the familiar voice, hoping it wouldn't cause her a delay. 'Hello Freddy, I'm really busy right now.'

Freddy was Paula's erstwhile husband, and although they got on well enough these days, he had a habit of taking the long way round of coming to a point. Being one quarter of an ageing rock band, with time on his hands during the daylight hours, he failed to recognise that other people had work to do.

'Don't be like that, Paula,' he said in a sulky little boy manner. 'I just thought I'd phone for a catch-up, but if you're busy, I'll leave it.'

Why did Freddy always make her feel like she was being unreasonable?

'If it's just a chat you're after, why don't you pop round later, to the house and we can catch up over supper and wine?'

'Great, I'll be there around seven, then, if that's OK?' replied Freddy, sounding much more cheerful.

'You'd better make it eight, Freddy. As I said I'm really pushed today. OK I'll see you later then,' said Paula.

After she put the phone down, Paula pinched the bridge of her nose. She felt irritated that she'd promised to entertain her ex-husband that evening. He had the knack of wrong-footing her like no one else. The man known as Freddy, his real name being Rob Fredericks, was not a bad person, but his lifestyle had driven her crazy over time. All the late nights, mild drug taking and general apathy, had resulted in them feeling out of sync with each other. After much soul searching, Paula decided an escape route was needed if she was ever going to progress in her life. She had too many things she wanted to achieve, and realised that, unfortunately, Freddy was holding her back. So the painful process of separation, followed by divorce was sadly inevitable.

Back in the moment, Paula fired up her computer, and took her notebook out of the desk drawer, reviewing the list of jobs she had to do that day. She felt a great sense of achievement working for herself, and loved, at the end of the day, to see a list, with all the tasks crossed through. She knew it was an old-fashioned way, as was her giant diary, but it worked for her. She did of course have to do a lot of work on her computer, but she also hung on to a few tried and tested methods. Gingham and Velvet had a trendy up-to-the-minute website which needed a lot of updating. They realised they needed a strong online presence and so paid quite a chunk of their hard-earned cash to Rory, a geeky friend of Nicky's daughter, Poppy, who was a real whizz on the computer. He had also, surprisingly, developed a keen interest in the latest fashion trends, so made it his business to pass on his observations to the two designers. It amused Nicky and Paula no end, but they had to admit it had proved pretty useful at times. As with many creative folk, they needed help with the business side of things.

After a while Nicky appeared with a bag of goodies which Paula munched her way through, and the two women worked in companionable silence for much of the rest of the day.

They had a few appointments in the diary over the next few days, clients coming in for fittings, one or two home visits, ongoing commissions to finish off and rep appointments to honour. In fact, Wednesday evening arrived much too swiftly for their liking.

Before leaving the barn, they zealously checked they had all the paraphernalia needed for the important commission.

After ticking everything off from their standard list for visits: fabric samples, tape measure, forms to be completed for their own files, and many other miscellaneous items, they set the alarm, locked the door and walked together towards their cars, having decided on their time of departure for the following day.

'Goodnight, Nicky. I'll see you in the morning. Have you decided on which pair of wonderful dungarees you're wearing tomorrow?' asked Paula, cheerfully.

'Oh no, I'll see what takes my fancy when I wake up.'

Paula looked at her friend fondly, taking in her slim frame, her unruly and thick brunette hair, which she chose to have cut regularly into a short messy mass of curls. Along with her cornflower blue eyes, which were always full of mischief, her fresh, freckled, open face, with its perfect nose and expressive mouth, Nicky was a tomboy through and through, and just as pretty as a picture.

They got into their respective cars, waving happily, and drove out of the car park, both unable to resist a last proud glance toward the barn, before setting off on their homeward journeys, eager for what tomorrow may bring.

CHAPTER TWO

'Mrs Armstrong,' called out Lady Soames for a second time. 'Where is that wretched woman?' she asked of no one in particular.

Lord Duncan and Toby, their younger son, made similar non-committal sounds, knowing there was little point in answering her question, yet both patently aware, with just those few spoken words, of the timbre creeping into her cadence.

Lord Soames, who spent most of his day sitting in the corner of the immense drawing room, stroking his moustache and sipping surreptitiously at his whisky, peeped out from behind his newspaper, and made a half-hearted attempt to pay attention to his wife, who had always been on the far side of difficult.

'I'm sure she will be along shortly, Philippa. She's always busily working away at something. Shall I pop into the kitchen and see?' he asked, obligingly, not relishing the thought of tracking down the housekeeper, but pacifying his wife had become such a common occurrence that he automatically offered to coerce.

'Yes, do that, please, Duncan. I need to discuss some menus with her.'

'Right you are, dear, I'll see what I can do.'

He rose from his favourite chair, folded his newspaper

neatly, placed it carefully back onto the faded, worn brown leather wing back chair, and vacated the room.

Glancing at her son, Lady Soames hesitated, wondering if her time would be best served in trying to quiz him once more about his present circumstances.

Toby had arrived home unexpectedly two days before, devoid of wife and children, from Africa where he worked in the oil industry. He had offered no reason as to why he'd unexpectedly pitched up at Starlington Hall. Both his parents had bombarded him with questions, but Toby remained resolutely guarded as to any kind of explanation, and had become agitated when pushed. He claimed jet lag and tiredness, promising to tell them his situation all in good time.

Would now be a good time, thought Philippa, who was not in the habit of pondering her decisions. But realising her younger son, who, when all was said and done, she was extremely fond of, had seemed so remote and unreachable these last few days, she felt nervous of upsetting him.

Thinking back, it was rather a shock when Toby bought his wife home for the first time.

He'd been working in Angola for a short time, living in the most expensive capital of the world, Luanda. When he returned to the UK for a holiday in the spring, he'd telephoned his parents from Heathrow airport, informing them he would be accompanied by his fiancée for the visit. His mother typically went into a spin, flabbergasted at the thought of an extra visitor, for whom she was not prepared, and extremely shocked that he had become engaged without informing them.

'How very characteristic it is of Toby to throw this upon us at the last minute. Should I tell Mrs Armstrong to prepare a guest room, or do you think they will expect to share a bedroom? Really, it's too bad of him to put us in this position,' she complained to her husband.

'Why don't you just wait until they arrive, and have a discreet word with Toby as to the state of play, Pip? Really, it's not a big problem. I'm rather looking forward to meeting our new daughter-in-law to be,' said Duncan, congenially, happy at the notion.

When, within a short time, they heard a car pull up at the front of the house, Philippa and Duncan walked into the vestibule together, eager to greet their son and his new fiancée, having hastily changed into fresh, smart clothes, and looking the picture of dignity and elegance.

If there had been a camera poised, waiting to capture the moment they met the newly betrothed couple, I wonder if it would have shown the level of astonishment witnessed.

'Hello, Ma and Pa,' greeted Toby. 'May I introduce you to Kellan?'

Duncan, taking a little longer than was polite, yet feeling rooted to the spot and unable to propel himself forwards any more rapidly, stepped into view, and managed to shake hands, followed, unevenly by Philippa.

Before them stood the most beautiful, noble, statuesque black woman they had ever seen. She was dressed in a traditional African outfit made from strong, bright, geometrical fabric. It was a stunning full-length dress, with a matching headband, adorned with coordinating heavy wooden jewellery. The overall result was quite breathtaking.

Toby noticed how the effect of his lovely bride-to-be was impacting on his parents, and felt fleetingly smug at being able to have shocked them so dramatically. He was unable to tell, at that stage, if they were more shaken by her colour or her beauty.

'How do you do, Lord and Lady Soames,' said Kellan, in a strong African accent. Even though she felt nervous meeting Toby's parents, she did, nevertheless, manage to portray a staggeringly confident manner.

Regaining her composure at a speedy rate, Lady Soames managed to locate her voice and gather her wits. 'How nice to meet you, Kellan,' she said. 'And what a pretty name you have. Is it an African name?'

Duncan shot an apologetic glance towards his son, but on seeing the beginnings of a smirk from Toby, gave him a quick wink, to let him know they were on the same page.

'Yes, it is. A typical African name, a family name, Lady Soames, used by my family for many generations,' went on Kellan, proudly, seemingly not insulted by the question.

'Oh well Kellan, now do please come with me, my dear. Can I offer you some light refreshments? You must be tired from your journey. I'll get Mrs Armstrong to bring us in a little something and we can begin to get to know one another,' she said smoothly, ushering Kellan into the drawing room, and lightly closing the door behind her.

'I'll help you with the cases, Toby,' volunteered Duncan, encouraging his son out of the front door towards the hire car. 'Well, that went rather better than I thought it might, truthfully. You certainly know how to shock your mother and me. This is a bolt out of the blue if ever there was one. I'm guessing you enjoyed that, you scallywag, and are probably just as staggered as I am at the way your mother handled it. What-what?'

'Honestly, Pa, yes I am! It just goes to show how the old girl can still surprise us both.'

'Is that an African name? Can you believe she actually said that,' he laughed.

This scene took place six years previously, and since that first meeting, Duncan and Philippa began to revel in spending time with their daughter-in-law, both in Angola and the UK, and secretly enjoyed seeing the look of amazement on the faces of their friends and family, on being introduced to the beautiful Kellan. They had both grown fond of her over time, and the twins, who were coming up to their fourth birthday, were both a joy and a delight to the proud grandparents. Now, looking towards Toby, she feared all was not well in Africa.

She sighed, but kept her counsel.

Vivienne Armstrong knocked on the door, breaking into Philippa's thoughts and bringing her back into the moment, then walked confidently into the room ready to face her employer. She handled Lady Soames very well, considering her disposition, and knew that as long as she was efficient at her job there could be no room for complaint.

Vivienne noticed a look of sadness about the eyes of Lady P today, and when they discussed the menus for the approaching week, there seemed to be an air of resignation and defeat to her. This was most unusual, and not at all what she'd been expecting after the hint of warning she'd had from Lord D of his wife's present mood. Vivienne felt sure it had something to do with the sudden appearance of Toby, and marvelled at the way a person could have such a dramatic change of mood, all in the space of fifteen minutes.

Vivienne and her husband, Colin, who was the gardener at Starlington Hall, always made a point of meeting up for morning coffee, and today was no exception.

Sitting at the big farmhouse table in the kitchen of the hall, having taken in the morning coffee to the family, relaxing now over a steaming cup of brew, and a plate of home-made shortbread, Vivienne relayed her thoughts to Colin.

'There's something "up" with Lady P, you mark my words, Col. She's not herself.'

'Go on with you, if anyone can make a mountain out of a molehill, it's my wife,' teased Colin. 'What's she got to be worrying over? I ask you, living in a place like this, with plenty of dosh in the bank, bossing everyone around, folks like you and me jumping to attention whenever she feels like it. She's got it made, what does she have to complain about?'

'I don't know, it's just a feeling I've got in me bones. I sometimes wonder how they manage to keep up with all the repairs and running costs of it all. Mind you, it's her money as funds it all, according to village gossip.'

'That's your trouble, Viv, you listen to way too much gossip in that post office. Anyway never mind about all that, what's on your agenda today? There's a strong wind blowing up out there today, so a good excuse, I'd say, for a nice early night tonight, cuddling up. I'll be chopping some more of them logs later, so I can get us a good roaring fire going, perfect for a romantic romp! What do you reckon?'

'Honestly, Colin, sometimes I wonder if that's all you think about. But now you come to mention it that sounds like a damn good idea.' Vivienne's eyes were twinkling mischievously as she glanced over at her well-built, handsome and virile husband. 'Come here, you brute.'

They embraced warmly, both knowing how much they still got turned on by each other.

Even after all the years together, their strong, loving relationship was as fresh as ever.

'Hey,' said Viv, drawing away from him, 'you'll have to wait until tonight for any shenanigans. I've work to do before that. I've to make lunch for a couple of dressmakers coming to fit Lady P out for her cruise. I'll need to pop into Romsey to buy some fresh fish first, so I'd better getting on, but hold onto that thought, big boy!'

Colin walked out of the kitchen, grinning to himself, and made his way to the old stable block. There were still a couple of hunters in the stables, ridden occasionally by both Lord D and Lady P, along with a few extra nags, some of which belonged to members of the local riding fraternity who required extra stabling. The walk was a pleasant one, and Colin looked round proudly at the profusion of crimson hues on the magnificent old trees which were as red as September. The sweeping lawns which he took great pride in, gave both trees and shrubbery a lush backdrop by which to show themselves off with, especially at this time of year.

Nearing his destination, he frowned when he noticed, in the distance, the door of the shed he'd commandeered as his own for housing his impressive motorbike, blowing about wildly in the wind. The rusty hinges were creaking, as they struggled to find the purchase to prevent from crashing and breaking away from the old wooden frame.

He increased his speed, running now, to save the door from ruin. Thankfully he managed to reach the shed before disaster struck. He placed the iron bars in to their structure firmly, thus averting a nasty bump to his bike.

'Who the hell has left those doors open?' he shouted at the top of his voice. Nobody could hear him, so he expected no reply, but had to give vent to his vexation one way or another. 'Bloody idiot, my bike could have been bloody well ruined.'

No one used this shabby, tumbledown shed, except for Colin, which is why he'd requested the use of it from Lord Duncan. He was puzzled as to why anyone would need to open the doors, let alone enter, and then neglect to close them properly on their way out. Whenever he worked on his bike, he had to be vigilant, making sure both doors were either closed firmly or securely held back.

He went inside now, and stood scanning his motorbike for signs of damage, or any alteration to its positioning. Walking around the bike to check thoroughly, he could detect no dent or scratch. It was out of harm's way now. Still pristine, even in the gloom of the old dark shed.

His usual warm brown, buttery smooth eyes, which normally showed a gentle glint, had changed to a fierce, dark brooding pair — screwed up tight. His face, which was flushed in anger, momentarily contorted menacingly. He loved his wife with a passion, but the Harley-Davidson came a very close second. If anyone had done any damage, he would not have liked to have been answerable for his actions. When he'd convinced himself that all was well, he started to think of a practical solution. He'd have to get a strong, large lock in place, so he set about searching for the tools he would need for the job.

There were a cluster of sheds and greenhouses which he frequented most of his working day, close to the stable block, containing all manner of odds and ends, so finding the tools was easy. He gathered them together swiftly in readiness for the work ahead. He had a strange feeling, though, that one or two of the boxes had been shifted around, maybe even tampered with. Making his way out of one of the sheds, with his head down, deep in thought, he heard a distinct thud in the nearby bushes.

He ran towards the bushes, shouting out as he went, but on searching the area found no signs of disruption, nor any culprit to account for the sound he felt sure he'd heard amongst the shrubbery.

There had been, in the past, a problem with poachers on the estate, so Colin thought it wise to inform Lord Duncan about his suspicions of an intruder.

Meanwhile, back at Starlington Hall, Duncan had taken up his position again on his chair, scanning the financial pages of his newspaper, whilst Philippa sat at her desk diligently studying her crossword.

'I was thinking,' ventured Duncan, timidly, 'maybe I'll spend a couple of days up in town next week.'

Philippa looked up from her crossword, peering at her husband above her reading glasses, which were perched on her nose, and now hastily pushed down. 'Please yourself, Duncan. I would have thought you may have stayed on home turf to lend some support to your son if needed, but if you feel the need to be off, then you go ahead.'

Duncan didn't feel inclined to respond, so hid once again behind his newspaper, letting out a small sigh of relief.

With a shake of the head as if a bee had just crossed her

vision, Philippa left the room.

Toby had driven one of the cars into the village, and was currently sitting on a bar stool, drinking a pint of real ale, feeling decidedly melancholy.

He didn't have an easy smile, in fact, his default setting inclined to morose. Having been brought up in the shadow of his elder brother, William, who wore a sunny smile without a struggle, and even though Toby was deemed to be the more successful, his forced joviality always appeared awkward. He was punctilious about hygiene and cleanliness, spending more time in the bathroom than many a woman, plucking stray hairs, applying spot cream and arranging his coarse head of flaxen hair. He wasn't a bad looking man, and prided himself on his strong set of arm muscles, and well-toned torso, but however hard he tried to move his very inviting lips into a naturally pleasant smile, they stubbornly refused to oblige. His eyes had a penetrating stare, and could change from grey to blue to almost black, depending on his mood. None of these details ever deterred members of the opposite sex from finding him strangely alluring. He never had difficulty in attracting women. They seemed to be fascinated by his moody "James Dean" persona.

He had got himself into something of a predicament in his life in Africa, which he didn't know how to resolve, and felt consumed by indecision. The facts kept rolling around in his head, causing sleepless nights and days of endless torment. He knew his parents would need to be told the truth soon, but was at a loss as to how he would manage the revelation.

CHAPTER THREE

Nicky and Paula were elated to be driving through the New Forest from their homes in Dorset. They passed seamlessly into the next county, as they both lived very close to the border. The ponies had their winter coats, and the heather, trees and scrub were still shrouded in the early morning mist as they travelled. Golden leaves cascaded down in front of their car, due to the windy conditions, creating a flurry of shimmering splendour as they drove. Nature needed no effort to show its beauty, no arranging, and no enhancement, just sun, rain and whatever the elements decreed. The friends agreed they would make more of an effort to spend time in the forest. Paula found inspiration with her paints and easel, and Nicky loved to walk her dog and take photographs. They were always looking for inspiration and were ever alert as to how they might incorporate the splendour of the natural world into their designs.

After a time of quiet contemplation, out of the blue, Paula spoke. 'Have you heard from Poppy lately?'

'Yes, well, she does send me the odd email, but the photos and most of the information reaches me through that darned Facebook to be honest. She's looking slim and tanned for sure, but I must say I wasn't too keen on the tattoo. The nose piercing was bad enough, but now she's gone and had a tattoo. What can I say, though, after all she is twenty? I'm just pleased she's still safe now that she's going it alone.'

Nicky's daughter, Poppy had set off on her delayed "gap year" having given up university after nearly two years, with her friend, Georgia. After a huge fallout in Australia, Georgia flew home and Poppy carried on by herself. She'd travelled to Fiji and Bali, then on to Thailand, where she was currently based, in Chiang Mai.

'She's having a great trip, Paula, but…'

Paula sensed a hesitation from Nicky, as if she was wrestling with something.

'What is it Nicky, what's the "but"?'

'Well, it's what I've been dreading. I told you about how she'd started asking me about her father didn't I? Well, she won't stop pestering me about him. She's like a dog with a bone,' Nicky trailed off, clearly finding it difficult to put into words.

'You have to tell her, Nicky, she has a right to know about him. You can't blame her for being curious, as you said, it was bound to come up one day.'

'But how can I tell her the truth about Christo?'

'For a start, you need to do it face to face. Why don't you just put her mind at rest and promise to tell her when she comes home?'

Nicky remained silent, ruminating over Paula's blunt words, sensing she was right, but still in a quandary of indecision.

'I know you're right. I'll give it some thought.'

Paula knew Nicky didn't like speaking or even thinking about this delicate matter, and realised it was best to drop the topic for the time being.

'How are we doing, Nicky, does the satnav say we have

far to go?'

Glancing up at the box of tricks, she replied 'Not much further. Twenty minutes to go.' Nicky was glad of the distraction.

'I feel a bit nervous. Excited, but nervous,' admitted Paula.

'It'll be a cinch, kitting Lady Soames out for her winter cruise, don't ya know?' quipped Nicky teasingly.

'It's her manner; she sounds like a real tyrant. I just hope we can pull it off.'

'No problem. Of course we can. Oh, by the way, I forgot to tell you, I've remembered where I know that Dr Antony Vickers from; it's my am-dram group. I've only met him a handful of times, three or four at the most. It beats me why he's recommended us. I took some of our cards into one of the rehearsals, a while ago. I can only assume he picked one up. Seemingly he was engaged to a local girl named Jessica, but she was killed in a road accident at the beginning of the year. How tragic, eh? He was in a bad way for a while, but it seems he's now taken up with one of her friends, according to Clodagh, who knows everything, of course!'

They continued the drive chattering away as they went, and a short time later Nicky spoke, 'Ah, here we are, two miles to Starlington Village. We'll be in the hamlet soon, and the house is about half a mile further.'

'Pretty countryside, I must say,' remarked Paula, looking round. 'I wish I could get rid of these butterflies in my stomach, though.'

Driving through the small, quaint Hampshire village they passed the regulation duck pond and public house, the large post office, a small parade of shops, including, obscurely, a

Lebanese restaurant, and out at the other end, where they spotted a sign showing the direction to Starlington Hall.

The road narrowed as they drove the rest of the way, and became bendier. Before long they caught sight of a set of colossal double wrought iron gates, with an impressive coat of arms cleverly incorporated, indicating they'd arrived at their destination.

The two women were stunned into silence when they passed through into the gated estate, and started to wend their way up the long sweeping driveway, flancked by trees and lawns of giant proportions on either side. They meandered along for quite some distance before getting their first glimpse of the magnificent house.

As they rounded the final corner, a figure came towards them, who quickly threw himself into the hedge, to avoid bumping directly into their vehicle, giving the women a start.

'Crikey, I could have run him over,' shouted Nicky, deftly swerving to avoid him. She braked suddenly, and was about to give him what for, but thought better of it, not wishing to cause a scene, and a bad start to the visit.

He'd had his head down, the collar of his green anorak pulled up as far as it would go, and was wearing a grey bobble hat. He looked scruffy, furtive and completely out of place. The girls looked towards his departing figure, puzzled, yet not surprised to see him gathering speed.

'There goes the "lone walker",' said Paula, and they both burst into giggles.

Paula and Nicky had a habit of giving people nick-names.

'Come on, we'd better calm down before we meet the

lord and lady, or we won't get the gig! We are serious business ladies from now on, remember.'

So, they parked up, took out their belongings, and made their way to the imposing front door.

A pretty, fresh faced lady with rosy cheeks and a pleasant smile opened the door.

'Hello, you must be the dressmakers. Welcome to Starlington Hall. Do come in, I'll take you to meet Lady Soames,' she said.

Nicky and Paula stepped inside the tall, dome-ceilinged vestibule, which was vast, and painted a duck egg blue, its intricate cornices picked out in white. The rosewood furnishings looked a little shabby, and the elaborate rug was quite worn in places, making the overall effect that of faded grandeur. It was still imposing, though, if somewhat noticeably and unpleasantly chilly.

Mrs Armstrong, the housekeeper, knocked lightly on one of the many doors leading from the hallway, and waited. When she heard a favourable response, she opened the door and ushered the two women inside.

'Ah,' spoke Lady Soames, rising from her chair, 'Gingham and Velvet I assume? Well, I'm glad to see you are on time. I trust you had a pleasant journey?'

'Yes,' agreed Paula, stepping towards Lady Soames, and shaking her hand, introducing herself, then Nicky, to their prospective new client.

Philippa Soames didn't give Paula the opportunity to say more before she carried on explaining the schedule she had in mind for the day.

'I thought we could get the business of the collection out of the way first, and any tedious stuff which you'll no doubt need to do, then we can partake of a late luncheon together. My husband and son will be joining us. I'm not one to fuss over my garments. I shall want plenty of changes of outfit; one does have to keep up appearances. But in all honesty, this dressing up every night can get extremely tiresome, which is why I chose to get it sorted out now, so I can get it packed away and then forget all about it. It's not like it would be my first choice of holiday, but we've been invited to join good friends for a special occasion, and quite frankly, I found it impossible to refuse.'

Both Nicky and Paula groaned inwardly, but had to concede that not everyone shared their own passion regarding style and flair.

Standing before them was a tall, slim upright woman, whom, they judged, was, in all probability, in her early sixties. She wore tweed slacks, a cream cashmere sweater with a turtleneck, and a padded gilet. Her fair upswept hair was styled in a French pleat, and diamond earrings her only jewellery. She had steely grey eyes and sharp features. She gave off an aura of respectability and authority.

'Do follow me up to my dressing room,' ordered Lady Soames, brusquely.

Nicky and Paula followed her out of the room, and mounted the staircase, both feeling like schoolgirls ordered to attend the headmistress's study.

They shot each other a look, and Paula realised she'd have to be courageous if they were to get any sort of respect, and a two-way relationship with this intimidating client.

On entering the dressing room, Paula, determined to be heard, started to disclose a little history about their company, but was told, in no uncertain terms by Lady Soames, just how disinterested she was in petty details, and would they please just, "get on with it".

Paula took a deep breath.

'We do pride ourselves in getting to know our clients in order to make our designs exclusively suited to them alone, Your Ladyship. We make bespoke, high-end garments,' she paused, catching her breath before proceeding. 'We would be most grateful if you might, therefore, take the time, so we can ensure we create a unique collection of garments, worthy of the Gingham and Velvet label. This is the way we always work,' she finished.

Philippa Soames was silent, digesting Paula's words, extremely unused to being spoken to in such a manner, yet starting to feel a grudging respect for the lady in front of her. She looked up from the dressing room stool, which she'd chosen to sit upon, and noticed Paula properly for the first time. She was very arresting.

'That was quite a speech, Mrs Fredericks. Very well, I will co-operate with you,' she said, with the beginnings of a repentant smile. 'Now, where do we start?'

From then on, Nicky took over the measurements, the perusing of the colour swatches and the completion of the questionnaire they had devised. Some of the questions were quite personal, and the women wondered if Lady Philippa would baulk, but in fact she seemed to be, albeit begrudgingly at first, starting to enjoy herself. Apart from the odd, "why on earth would you need to know what kind of music I enjoy?" she behaved and co-operated beautifully. They then looked through her wardrobe together, and asked her to pick her three favourite items.

Lady Soames took a little time to decide, and her three

choices were quite surprising, especially one in particular. It was an eye-catching summer coat which had some very unusual fastenings on it, and looked more like something Paula may choose to wear herself.

'Paula held the coat at arm's length, and asked, 'Would you mind if we hang on to this one, Lady Soames?'

'Oh, do call me Philippa. It drives me mad, all this formality. Yes do hang on to any one you choose, if it will help. We'll need to get a move on, though, as we're in danger of being late for luncheon. Are we nearly finished?'

'Yes, we have everything we need for now, but will need to arrange a date for your first fittings at a later stage,' replied Nicky.

'That's fine, but now we must make our way to the dining room. We can discuss further plans over lunch. I have actually rather enjoyed myself you know,' she said a tad sheepishly.

'I'm so pleased to hear that, Lady, erm, sorry, Philippa. We do want to get it right for you,' said Paula, feeling uncomfortable at the use of her client's first name.

They descended the staircase, all feeling much more relaxed.

Mrs Armstrong was waiting in the hallway, trying not to show that she was a little put out at their slight lateness.

When they had been shown into the dining room, Lady Philippa asked Paula and Nicky if they would care to partake of an aperitif before luncheon.

They were then introduced to Lord Duncan and Toby, who were pleased to note that Lady P seemed to be in good humour, and so, all now sipping the fine dry sherry, they stood making small talk until they were shown to their seats at the dining table.

Nicky and Paula were now on first name terms with the family, and felt able to hold their own during the meal, where Lord Duncan, in particular, seemed genuinely interested to hear all about their fledgling business. Toby lost his dour look, and moreover made a sterling effort to make the two amiable guests feel welcome, so all in all the luncheon party was proving successful.

The food was delicious, a home-made parsnip and apple soup, followed by a tasty fish pie. Mrs Armstrong was generous with the pouring of the wine, though Nicky declined, holding her hand over her glass to indicate this, as she would need to drive back, and had already drunk a rather large glass of sherry.

As the drinks flowed, everyone began to relax a little more, and by the time the dessert was served, a chocolate torte with cream, the talk had become quite animated. They chatted about the forthcoming cruise to the Mediterranean, and about some of the places they would be visiting when going ashore. They both seemed to be focused on the city of Lisbon for some reason, as if that was to be the highlight of the trip. All was going well, until, that is, Lady Philippa, bolstered by one too many glasses of wine, decided to tackle the subject, once more, of why Toby had come home unexpectedly.

There was a tight silence, and a tension in the air, as Toby glared at his mother, his father stared down at his plate, clearly embarrassed, and Toby lost his temper.

'How typical of you, Mother, to bring up a difficult subject in front of guests. Do you think I'm going to be drawn into your little ploy? Do you really believe I'm going to tell these nice ladies all my secrets, eh?'

'Stop it, Toby. Don't be so rude,' replied Philippa, immediately, adding fuel to the fire.

'Oh, I'm rude am I? Well, bad luck, Mother. I will not be hounded or goaded by you or anyone. I'll tell you when I'm good and ready, and let that be an end to it.' With that, he stood up, scraped his chair back abruptly, slung his napkin on the table and left the room.

Everyone sat in silence for a minute, before Lord Duncan spoke.

'I'm so sorry you had to be witness to that, ladies, there's no excuse for the way my son behaved. But,' he said, turning towards his wife, 'really, Philippa, you do choose your moments.'

'I think we'd better be making a move now, anyway, don't you think, Paula? We don't want to get caught up in the traffic on the M27. It can get very heavy at certain times,' put in Nicky, the only sober voice in the room.

'Yes, we'd better be making tracks,' agreed Paula.

'You really don't have to rush off, you know,' put in Philippa, in a small voice.

'That's kind, Philippa, but as I said, the traffic could be a problem if we leave it any longer. Thank you so much for a lovely meal, and giving us so much useful information.' She stood up and pushed her chair away from the table, swiftly followed by a wine-induced, red-cheeked Paula.

'Yes, thank you for your kind instructions, and delicious meal, Philippa. We will look forward to meeting you again soon. I'll telephone you to discuss a time, when we've made headway with the designs and patterns,' said Paula.

Lord Duncan and Lady Philippa stood up, both looking

rather crestfallen at having their luncheon party cut short, especially knowing the circumstances which had caused it.

They all walked into the vestibule, feeling somewhat awkward, but managed to shake hands and depart in a civil manner. Although the two women were relieved to be leaving after the embarrassing scene at the dining table, they also felt satisfied at having been able to have secured such a lucrative order from their new client.

Nicky started the engine, and slowly began to drive away from the main house.

'You see,' said Paula, 'however much money you have, it doesn't guarantee happiness does it, Nicky? There must be something pretty grave going on, for Toby to have reacted so strongly. Mind you, it was a bit tactless of his mother, whose new name, by the way, is Lady Lizbum, as she's so keen to get to Lisbon. Oh and did you notice how Lord Duncan can't leave his moustache alone, he's always twizzling and stroking it... he's got to be The Twizzler!'

'Paula, you're impossible!' laughed Nicky.

'You see, though Nicky — no one knows what goes on behind closed doors.'

'Hmmm, let me see, yes, Charlie Rich wasn't it? Around 1973 I think you'll find,' finished Nicky, as quick as a whip.

CHAPTER FOUR

In stark contrast to their country residence, the apartment belonging to Lord and Lady Soames was modern and functional. The interior had plain walls throughout, painted white, with modern furniture and sanded floorboards, giving a feeling of space and minimalism. A few carefully placed pieces of art deco, and tasteful paintings, in keeping with the style of the period in which it was built, were its only relief from plainness. It had been bought at a time when property prices were relatively low, yet was now worth well above the typical market price in the capital, due to its location, in an area of London vastly desirable to the discerning buyer.

There had been many heated discussions recently between Lord and Lady Soames as to whether they should keep hold of the apartment in Pimlico Court, with Philippa keen to sell, and Duncan being adamant about not wanting to. The maintenance costs had escalated in recent years. Lady Soames, realising that her beloved Starlington Hall was a bottomless pit in terms of running costs, and being the more pragmatic of the two, felt sure they should sell the apartment and sink the money into their country pile.

Although Duncan was a mild-mannered man, he could also be very stubborn.

He had been born into a wealthy family, so never felt the need to be overly ambitious. Having been assured by his father that he would never be without funds, he'd drifted into work at the Home Office for the want of anything better to do with his time. He found he enjoyed London; he liked the buzz of city life. He became a member of a gentleman's club, and appreciated many things, including art galleries and cultural venues. For him the apartment felt like a vital part of his existence, even though he was now retired. His wife, on the other hand, having had an extraordinarily privileged upbringing as part of the aristocracy, and having been left an inordinate amount of money over the years, by various obscure relatives, unquestionably favoured the country life. Duncan knew, though, that she would miss the theatre and the tempting stores in the capital if they abandoned the unique and valuable second home. It rankled, therefore, that she would even consider selling.

It was his bolthole.

He stood behind the kitchen worktop, which divided the small kitchen from the ample, open-plan sitting and dining area, and poured himself a generous shot of whisky, topping it up with dry ginger, and plopping in a couple of ice cubes from the freezer. Then, carrying it through to the lounge, he placed it on the coffee table, sitting down and stretching out his long legs in one easy movement.

'Ah,' he thought. 'Peace at last.'

Duncan was an orderly man. His eyes, as blue as a winter ocean, still had a sparkle about them and his hair, although now quite white, was gentle and fluffy, framing a distinguished face with a cautious mouth, curtained by a luxuriant moustache. He dressed in traditional clothes, cavalry twill trousers, muted check shirts and sports jackets being his preferred attire.

His schedule for the next few days was mapped out with precision, as was his habit. Tonight he would be making his way to a restaurant along the water's edge of the Thames, to meet his older son, William. Deciding on a whim, that he would have a change to his usual outfit, he departed to the bedroom.

William stepped nonchalantly from his vessel onto the gangplank, and then walked onto the towpath. He knew he was late for the planned rendezvous with his father, yet did not feel in the least bit concerned. Adopting his usual sloping, casual pace, and stopping for a chat with one or two of his colourful neighbours, he eventually arrived at the chosen venue.

Duncan jumped up immediately and raised his hand to beckon William, then with his other, summoned the waiter over to order drinks.

'Hello, Will, what's your poison tonight, son?' he enquired.

'Hello Pa, I'll have a pint of Guinness, please,' replied William.

When the waiter had left for the bar, Duncan gave William a hearty hug, and then they both sat down, and studied each other.

'You've put on a bit of weight, I see,' teased Will. 'What's the word, Pa? Portly is it?'

'I'll have you know I'm no different from when I saw you last, if you don't mind. Hmmm, it must be this wretched waistcoat. I got talked into purchasing it recently by my tailor. He assured me it was just the thing to make me look a bit trendier.'

'I think he saw you coming, Pa. Do you still go to Linton

and Linton?'

'Yes, I damn well do, perhaps I'd better change my allegiance.'

'No, Pa, don't do that. You look spiffing, I'm just pulling your leg.'

'You rotter! Now, let me have a good look at you. Well, you're certainly not looking portly. Are you eating enough? Your mother always wants to fatten you up.' He surveyed the handsome face of his elder son, taking in the mop of curly mid-brown hair, his angular symmetrical features, and hazel eyes rimmed with grey, under strong brows. He had a longish nose and straight mouth around which grew thick dark stubble. 'You had better go for the steak and kidney pudding tonight, Will.'

'Pa. I don't believe it. I do make allowances for Ma, but you, I thought I'd drummed it into your head long ago. I don't eat animals, I'm a vegetarian. Remember?' Will said, with a touch of sarcasm.

'Will, I'm so sorry, son, of course you are. It just slipped my mind in the moment; my memory isn't what it was. Would you forgive an old man?'

William gave a little sigh, but went on to say, 'OK, not a problem, Pa. Come on then, we'd better study the menu, that waiter looks ready to pounce.'

After placing their order, the two men chatted amiably, happy to be in each other's company. Duncan saw William more than he let on to Philippa, as she found it hard to reconcile herself to Will's lifestyle. She saw him as a drifter and a waster, as he lived on a canal boat and earned his money by being a street artist. Although he got quite a kick from drawing caricatures, and had a natural talent for observation, which was key, his real passion was writing. He worked doggedly on his manuscript which he hoped one day would be worthy of publication. His mother had no understanding or patience with his way of life, a vegetarian who frequently visited ashrams in the Far East, and practised Buddhism, yoga, and meditation. He had no long-term relationship, but was happily single, with plenty of friends, and was, above all, a contented man.

'How is Toby faring?' asked William.

'To be honest, Will, I was glad to escape for a while. The atmosphere has become untenable. When are you seeing him? If anyone can get some sense out of him, it'll be you.'

'I've spoken to him on the phone, but he's evasive about making a firm date. It's not like him, we've always been so open with each other, as you know, but he's holding something back. Ma's asked me to come on the weekend of the shoot. It's not my idea of fun, shooting at breathing targets just for the "sport", but I can occupy myself elsewhere on the estate I suppose.'

'Oh yes, Will, do please say you'll come.'

'Well, if Toby doesn't come up to London in the meantime, I'll definitely be there.'

Duncan thanked Will profusely, and they changed the subject, speaking about all manner of diverse topics, both content to spend time together. The evening drew to a close, and father and son departed, each to his own way of life.

The following day, Duncan made tracks to his club, unexpectedly bumping into one of his best friends, Richard Vickers.

'Hey, Duncan, what are you doing here? I didn't know

you were in town. Why, you should have let me know, old boy. Are you dining alone?'

'Yes, I am, though not here,' replied Duncan, a little warily. 'Bit of a spur of the moment decision to come up to town, don't you know?'

'I'm meeting a couple of pals, but I'm sure they wouldn't mind an extra one, old boy. Decent enough chaps, from the old firm as a matter of fact. I'll have a word with young Gregory and see if he can lay us up an extra place.'

'Oh, no need, old chap. As I said, I wasn't thinking of eating here, I just called in for a quick dram. I need to do a bit of food shopping. Bit of a cock up on the catering front, I need to get in fresh supplies. I just thought I'd fortify myself before I face the dreaded food hall in M&S. I'll grab a sandwich when I return to the apartment.'

'Well, if you're not dining here, Duncan, you must come tonight, for supper. Helen would never forgive me if I didn't extend an invitation to you whilst you're up in town,' said Richard cordially.

Duncan hesitated before replying, feeling uncomfortable in the extreme, and kicking himself for not being able to pass by the blasted club without entering.

'So very kind of you, old boy, but I'm afraid I can't take you up on your kind offer. I have a prior engagement.'

Richard felt a tad put out by his friend's evasiveness, but felt disinclined to make further enquiries, as Duncan had made it quite clear he wasn't about to divulge his plans.

'All right, Duncan, we'll have to make it another time then? I'm sure the ladies will have some scheme in mind, eh, what?'

'Ah, yes, don't forget the shoot is coming up soon at the

hall. I'll look forward to seeing the two of you then, if not before, Richard,' he said, draining the rest of his drink, offering his hand to shake, and departing quickly.

Richard watched his chum walking towards the door, with a puzzled look on his face.

'Phew,' thought Duncan, as he headed off in the direction of Marks and Spencer's. 'That was a close call.'

Sitting at the makeshift dressing table, in a seedy, damp, disappointing room, on the other side of the city, sat a disillusioned young lady. She took a long drag from the joint which had been resting in the ashtray, holding her head back, lolling it against the hard wooden chair back, and letting the smoke out slowly, in one long breath, creating a fine grey line. She didn't feel inclined to start the gruelling chore of getting ready for tonight's performance. She wanted to curl up in her narrow, single bed, and sleep for hours on end, to block out the reality of what her life had become, but she knew that was impossible.

She made herself sit up and started to apply the thick make-up over her bony face, layer upon layer, building it up like a mask, then, paying special attention to the eyes, she picked up her tweezers and carefully squeezed out a thin line of glue onto her oversized false lashes and fixed them on her eyelids, expertly. The dark brown powder, followed by the black eye liner was next, then mascara which helped to blend the false lashes with her real, sparse ones. She drew a thick line over her thin eyebrows with a harsh black pencil, brushing them out to her satisfaction, and then finished the whole, provocative look, with a purple lipstick.

She brushed out her straggly straight hair, and attached

the blonde hairpiece, wincing when the hairgrips dug into her scalp, but knowing she had to make her hair lustrous, to complete her signature look. Most of the girls at the club sat in a line, before the performance, in the dingy, dark space which the management called a dressing room, putting on their make-up together, laughing, chatting, and catching up on the latest gossip. She preferred to do it alone, however, not wanting anyone else to know how she looked without her screen. They saw her as an enigma, and she knew she came across as aloof, but that was not her concern, she just wanted to do her job and keep a low profile.

She sat quietly in the back of the regular black cab she used, with her eyes closed. The cabbie dropped her off at the back of the notorious Soho club. She walked confidently on, nodding to the burly security guard as she past him, and in through the back stage door.

Sitting at his solitary table, Lord Soames stroked his moustache with trembling fingers, waiting in anticipation for the familiar music to strike up, and the exquisite sight of the burlesque chorus girls to appear. He sipped at his whisky, picked at the snacks in front of him, savouring the thought of what lay ahead, beginning to feel a stirring in his loins.

When the music started, and the curtain parted, his eyes immediately found the object of his desire, and he watched, spellbound, as she danced erotically, in his eyes, just for him. He knew he would disappear at the end of the evening into a darkened room at the back of the theatre to be with her once more, as he had done on many previous occasions. He was well and truly under her spell.

When she saw Duncan making his way towards the side

door, which was known only to a few well-heeled patrons, she knew what was in store. She slipped down to the basement and into the dungeon, with its well-stocked equipment. She started to get together all his favourite toys. He made it easy for her, and was a soft-hearted man, unlike some of the other punters, so she felt relaxed and confident at what lay ahead. Most importantly, he always paid well above the going rate.

Duncan knocked tentatively, and when she opened the door to him, and they were in close proximity, he seemed to lose all sense of reason. He was putty in her hands.

The persona she adopted came naturally. She loved being a dominatrix, and was one of the best in the business. She enjoyed the feeling of power she wielded. She looked him up and down, her eyes piercing him to the very core.

After a series of orders, and when she felt he was sufficiently humiliated, she gave her final command.

CHAPTER FIVE

On their return from Hampshire, Nicky and Paula needed to be diligent. They had to concentrate on the collection for Lady Philippa after initially completing all other unfinished orders. Paula was realistic about not taking on any new business for the time being. She was diplomatic and engaging on the telephone, and Nicky constantly admired her buddy for the way she handled the work schedule.

They both knew this commission may guide them towards a more prominent set of clientele if handled well, and ultimately ensure that the Gingham and Velvet label became elevated to a higher position in the world of haute couture.

They got busy with the sketches and Nicky had even started on the slopers in calico, for a few of the more formal garments. Lady Lizbum had primarily requested seven evening gowns, including one for a gala dinner. She'd also need daytime outfits for their spells on terra firma, and a range of items for life on board the ocean liner. Although most of their usual assignments involved cutting edge bespoke fashion design, they were also mindful of the mode of client they were dealing with on this occasion. They would need to tone down some of their more radical ideas. As they didn't charge their client by the hour, the vast amount of fabrics, zips, buttons, cotton and many other sundry items all had to be laboriously accounted for and calculated with precision, before they could begin to work out profit margins, and arrive at a final figure. This task lay well and truly in the hands of Paula, as Nicky got completely carried away with the delight of creating, without much of a thought for the budget.

Even though Paula was pushed for time, she had an unexpected telephone call which made her heart sing. Her daughter, Tegan, was making a flying visit to the barn, from London, whilst visiting Dorset, on one of her itinerant visits.

In she breezed, armed with a box full of cream cakes, setting it down dangerously close to a drawing which her mother was working on, concentrating hard and puzzling over what kind of a neckline to give her client. In typical fashion, Tegan picked up the nearest pencil and drew in a perfect sweetheart neckline on the half-finished sketch.

'Hey, you, what the hell do you think you're doing?' asked a shocked Paula, swinging round in her chair to face her daughter.

'You've got to admit it, Mum, it looks pretty damn good, eh?' Tegan said, planting a kiss on her mother's cheek, and standing back to admire her handiwork.

'Go on, I bet you were going to give her a square neck, weren't you?'

'Know it all!' smiled Paula, knowing that she was absolutely right. 'Come here, you irritating child and give your mum a hug.'

Tegan was just about everything that Paula had always wished to be. The word fearless was invented for her daughter. She had always been a spirited child, with an inquisitive and probing nature. She was an impish pixie with the energy of a sprite.

'Hello, Auntie Nicky. Am I right, or am I right?'

Nicky, not wanting to be drawn into any kind of dispute between mother and daughter, thought it incumbent to change the subject, so launched into an accepted and tested one.

'Hey, Tegan, how's it going for you? What's new in the world of music?'

Tegan planted a kiss on the cheek of her favourite adopted aunt and regaled them both with a précis of how it was to be the assistant editor on a famous music magazine. It was mesmerising and shocking how confident Tegan was. The two women listened keenly to tales of showbiz scandal and musical gossip experienced by Tegan on a daily basis.

She had fallen into her job effortlessly, as the result of Freddy's status as a famous, albeit a few years down the road, popular and influential rock star. She was regularly photographed by the paparazzi, falling out of nightclubs in London in the early hours, looking the worse for wear, characteristically shrugging off any attempt to rearrange herself. Because she truthfully had no desire for fame, she'd become a firm favourite with the press.

One of the reasons the paparazzi loved her so much was because of her disregard of authority, and convention. A self-confessed bisexual, she showed no remorse for the outrageous way she behaved.

She had startling big green eyes, the same round shape as Freddy and titian locks inherited from Paula. Her short spiky hair was cut expertly into a quirky elfin style. Tegan's mode of dress was unconventional. She typically sported a nifty little hat or similar along with an ensemble which always erred on the side of wacky. It was sometimes downright weird, but oddly, at all times spot on. Paula never knew what her daughter would wear, or do, from one day to the next. She'd learned to accept the unexpected, and when she was around her daughter, she felt like a breath of fresh air and joy had wafted into her sphere. She loved her unconditionally.

'Darling, look, we're really pushed with an order here. Be a love, let yourself in at home, and I'll join you later.' Paula pushed her door keys towards her daughter knowing she needed to crack on. 'We'll get a takeaway tonight, and have a proper catch-up.'

'No sweat, Mum, I'll call in on Dad, and see you later,' replied Tegan, strutting towards the door with a huge cake stuffed into her mouth, spilling out double cream onto her chin, as she sashayed her way out of the barn.

Nicky and Paula didn't talk much for the next few hours, firstly shell-shocked by the burst of energy in the tranquil barn, and then needing to concentrate again on the job in hand.

Working until the early evening had become the norm for them both, and when Nicky started to pack away her paraphernalia, ready to call it a day, Paula was happy to do the same.

'I'm calling in on my dad on the way home. I'm a bit baffled by the way he's behaving. He seems to have something on his mind. I'm so worried he may be ill,' Nicky confessed.

Paula looked up, startled at this news.

'Surely not, love. Leonard's as strong as an ox.'

'Well, you say that, but there's something amiss, and I

intend to get to the bottom of it.'

Paula felt a sense of foreboding, knowing how much Nicky loved and relied on her father, and hoped with all her heart that she was wrong about her suspicions. Her mother, Caroline, had died when Nicky was just three years old, and Leonard had bought her up single-handed, so along with her daughter, Poppy, he was the closest family Nicky had.

Leonard saw the familiar car pulling into the curb, from his chair which was placed in the bay, near the window in his front room. He'd been on the lookout for his daughter, having come in from his garden, where he'd been cutting down some shrubs in readiness for winter. He was a keen gardener, and spent many happy hours tending his plants. He lived in a modest bungalow, in a quiet cul-de-sac. Leonard was dressed now in a dark navy blazer, grey flannels and a highly polished pair of shoes, having changed out of his scruffy gardening gear. He led a life of discipline even though he was now retired from the army, where he'd served most of his time in Africa. As was the habit of most military men, he ran a tight ship; he had his routine, and rarely deviated from it. He enjoyed a few pints at the local pub with his cronies, who were ex-army officers, local business men and members of the local council, in the main.

He watched his beloved daughter walk down the path to the front door, which he opened before she had a chance to ring the bell.

'Hello, and how's my best girl?' he asked, sincerely, leading her inside.

'Hi, Dad, I'm good,' replied Nicky. 'But more to the point, how are you?'

Nicky looked into her father's eyes, conveying her concern.

'Me? I couldn't be better; I'm fine, just fine.'

'Are you really, Dad? Only, I get a sense that there's something worrying you.'

Leonard carried on, putting the kettle on to boil, reaching for the mugs from the kitchen cupboard, and locating the packet of biscuits he'd purchased especially for Nicky. He wasn't much of a cook, but always made sure he had a little treat for his daughter, as he enjoyed making a fuss of her.

He waited until the tea was brewed and poured, the biscuits set out neatly on their plate, and then proceeded to carry the tray through to the compact lounge, before speaking.

Making up his mind to get straight to the point, he stated 'I've had an email from Poppy.'

'Yes, so have I, Dad. I had one only this morning. When did you receive yours?' she asked anxiously.

'Oh, it was last week as a matter of fact.' Leonard hesitated before going on, nervous over how to broach the subject with his daughter.

'The thing is, darling, the thing is, you see...'

'Come on, out with it, Dad, for goodness' sake.'

'Yes. I must. Well, the truth is, she's asking me about her father, and I don't know what to tell her,' he burst out.

Nicky looked down at the biscuit she was about to eat, stunned into silence.

'That's not fair, Dad. She shouldn't have brought you into this,' said Nicky, quietly.

'The point is, Nicky, she's got a right to know. I've never interfered, as you know, but the girl is an adult now and she's bound to be curious. It's been bothering me, not knowing how to reply to her, and I hadn't wanted to trouble you, but, well, there it is. You need to have a think and advise me how to reply to my grandchild. I'll not be lying, though, I can tell you that much.'

Nicky looked out of the bay window and let out a big sigh.

'I would never ask you to lie to your grandchild Dad. I've decided I need to have a long talk with Poppy about this, and tell her the truth when she returns, so I'd appreciate it if you could simply reiterate that to her in your reply.'

'All right, thanks, darling. I'll do that. Let's just drop it for now, anyway, and talk of something else.'

They both felt easier, especially Nicky, who was mightily relieved that her dear dad had no mystery illness looming.

A few days later, and after another demanding day in the barn, Nicky returned to her Victorian semi on the edge of the village. The house needed some serious renovation work done to it. It was a bit tired and shabby, tidiness not being high on Nicky's list of priorities. There was a catalogue of jobs she'd love to be getting on with, but there never seemed to be enough spare cash or time to start them. She had a long garden, where her big shed stood, and now that Gingham and Velvet had moved to the barn, Nicky hadn't taken long to fill it again. Photography equipment, incomplete costumes for the latest production, half finished "up-cycling" projects, and a general dumping ground for all manner of sports kit and sundry items was clearly its new purpose.

After a quick and simple meal of pasta with pesto sauce,

she had a frantic search for her script, before departing again, this time to drive into Christchurch town centre, to the car park of the hall which was the meeting place of the 'am-dram'. She arrived as she always did, a bit flustered and at the last minute, offering her apologies.

She found herself sat next to Dr Antony Vickers, so as soon as she was able to, in the break between scenes, she thanked him for his recommendation.

He looked a bit puzzled at first, and then remembered how it had come about.

'Ah, yes,' he said. 'Actually it was Lisa, my girlfriend, who picked up your card, so I can't take full credit. It was a chance conversation with her about the cruise for my parents' fortieth wedding anniversary. Duncan and Philippa Soames, as you probably know, will be joining them, and I mentioned that Pip was looking for a good dressmaker. Lisa remembered you'd left some of your business cards here, so she produced one, and I just passed it on. So, in all honesty, it's her you really need to thank. She'll be along later. I'll introduce you.'

'Yes, please do. It's a first-rate order for us, and we're very grateful.'

Before long Lisa arrived in the hall, and quickly made her way over to Antony, who, true to his word, introduced her to Nicky.

'Thank you so much for remembering about our card, Lisa. It was certainly a stroke of luck for us,' said Nicky, pleasantly.

'Ah yes, for Lady Soames. Oh well, I hope you can manage to please Her Ladyship, although that may be a bit of a tall order, if you know what I mean? Rather you than me I must say. I expect it will be quite lucrative for you, though, at least.'

Nicky was a little taken aback, detecting a distinct coolness to her tone. She was shocked at this, and started to wonder if she'd regretted giving Anthony their card. Why did she bother in the first place?

'Yes, we've met up with Lady Soames, and have started on the designs, which are coming along nicely. We'll give it our best shot. I'd like to think we'll do a good job,' said Nicky, a tad defensively.

'I'm sure you will, Nicky. I'm sorry, I didn't mean to put you off. Have you been invited to the shoot by the way?'

'Yes, we have, as a matter of fact. We're going to combine the visit with some fittings, and I understand Lady Soames will be happy for us to make up the numbers on the weekend. We're quite looking forward to it actually. Will you be there?'

'Yes. Antony always attends when he can, and I thought I might tag along.'

'Right, well, I'll see you there then. I must be getting along now, I've another early start in the morning. Goodbye to you both,' Nicky concluded.

The following morning, Nicky told Paula about her encounter.

'I met Antony Vickers and his girlfriend, Lisa last night. It seems she's the one who picked up our card and recommended us. Antony just passed the card to Lady Lizbum. She was quite rude about Philippa to start with and then in the next breath she seemed to change her mind. Anyway you'll meet her at the shoot.'

'I can't wait! Anyway, that's as maybe, but it's working out well for us, so I suppose we should be grateful to her.'

'Hmmmm, yes I suppose so.'

'What's she like?'

'She's very thin and willowy and looks like a feather would knock her over, she could easily be a model in fact. She's attractive in a "waiflike" way if you like that kind of look. Rather pale, with high cheekbones. Yes, we could call her The Waif.'

'I like that, Nicky, "The Waif". Ah well, it takes all sorts. Hey, by the way, have you seen these fancy toggle things on this coat of Lady Lizbum's? They look like little people.' Paula took the summer coat over to where Nicky was sitting.

'I did notice them, yes, but let's have a better look.'

The two women examined the fasteners, turning them over and studying the backs.

'Look, there's something on the back of this one, it looks Japanese, or at least oriental in some way.'

'How very unusual they are. We'd better take care not to damage any. Have we finished with the coat now? Will we be returning it on the next visit, or do you need to hang onto it for it a bit longer?'

'We can take it back on the weekend of the shoot, I don't need it any more.'

They carried on working into the early evening.

When Paula was driving down the familiar roads after work, on her way home, she began to feel butterflies in her stomach. For a little while now, she'd had a secret lover. He'd answered her advertisement for a gardener, and when he turned up on her doorstep on that first day, her heart had skipped a beat. The chemistry had been so strong, neither of them could ignore it, so before long, and against her better judgement, they had started a passionate affair. He was thoroughly unsuitable, and they both knew it wasn't going to be a committed relationship. He was separated from his young wife, who had been the one to initiate the break from her husband, and so at the present time he lived with his mother. He was much younger than Paula. It was her best kept secret, and she had every intention of keeping it that way. She especially kept it from Freddy, who she knew, still held a bit of a torch for her. She had no desire to come between her lover and his wife. She even encouraged him to return to her and his children from time to time. He'd needed a listening ear, and she was a good listener, gently pointing things out from a woman's perspective, and never placing his wife in a bad light. She knew one day he would return to the family home, and was prepared to let him go when the time came. But for now he was undeniably her guilty pleasure, and she made the most of their snatched liaisons, by blissfully living in the moment together.

She arrived home and pulled onto the driveway of her Edwardian villa. Paula alighted from her vehicle and stepped into her unusual and striking hallway. She walked on the mosaic tiled floor to the well-appointed kitchen, where she poured herself a large glass of red wine.

She climbed the stairs and entered the bathroom. There she placed her glass on a handy ledge ready to enjoy, put the plug into the bath and turned on the ornate taps. She poured in a generous amount of musky smelling bath cream and lit the candles surrounding the majestic bath. When everything was prepared to her satisfaction, and she was naked, she climbed in and sank back in the luxurious warmth, reaching for the glass of wine.

Anticipating what lay ahead, she couldn't stop a seductive smile from forming on to her sensuous lips…

CHAPTER SIX

Vivienne and Colin Armstrong were fully engrossed in the preparation for the annual shoot weekend which was drawing ever closer. Lord and Lady Soames, whilst keeping a tight hold on the purse strings, recognised the need to employ extra staff from the village over the preceding week, and the weekend itself. Vivienne needed help with the room preparations, the general cleaning and catering, whilst Colin would be required to organise the beaters, and their dogs.

They'd had several years' experience of this, but each year, with a new crop of helpers, the outcome varied a great deal.

The house itself was quite spread out and confusing for any visitor, notably on the first floor, and Vivienne was meeting with her employer today to discuss room allocation.

As in previous years, they were hosting an "Eight-gun shoot", four of whom were participants from surrounding villages and locale, who would not be residing at the hall, merely being present at the hall on the days of the shoot itself, and attending the banquet.

Lady P was sitting in her preferred battered pink velvet, buttoned chair in the drawing room, opposite Vivienne, who was perched on the edge of a Knole settee and had a notebook and pen poised ready to take instructions. The room was dominated by a chimney piece carved in marble and alabaster. Pendant plasterwork decorated the ceiling and elaborately carved panelling covered the walls. Upon these walls hung life-sized portraits of past generations, gazing down in an assortment of poses and attires.

'My son, William, will of course sleep in his usual room, in the east wing. He is bringing a guest, a Miss Phoebe Granger, who we will put in the blue room,' stated Lady P. 'Richard and Helen Vickers can have their usual one, the Gainsborough, opposite my dressing room. Antony, and his companion, whose name escapes me...'

'I think its Lisa Moore, Lady Philippa, if it's the same one who came with him to the summer barbecue?' put in Vivienne.

'Ah, yes, that's right, Mrs Armstrong. What a good memory you have. It's such a pity what happened to Jessica, his fiancée. I was rather fond of her, but I can't say I took to this latest one, however, these things take time I suppose...' Philippa looked through the window, into the far distance, a particular recollection suddenly resurfacing out of the blue, momentarily causing her to lose focus. Then she sharply brought herself back into the present, picking up on the job in hand. 'Yes, they can go in the room next door at the top of the stairs, the Constable room.'

'That just leaves the ladies from Gingham and Velvet, who will be given the large twin-bedded room. The floral room will suit them nicely.'

'All of those guest rooms are in the west wing. We're not expecting the remaining four gentlemen to be staying over, but I suppose you'd better make up another couple of rooms just in case. We know Mrs A, do we not, from past experience how messy things can get? Most will have chauffeurs, of course, but, it's best for us to be prepared. So, yes, make up the beds in the green and the grey rooms.'

'Very well, Lady Philippa,' said Vivienne after making a note of the directives, and rising from her chair.

'No need to rush off, Mrs Armstrong, I want to ask you about the help this year. How are they shaping up?'

'No problems so far, I'm glad to report. Most of them came last year, so they have an idea of what's expected. Mrs Barnes has bought along her daughter, Verity, for the first time. She seems to have her head screwed on, but I hope she won't get distracted when the beaters arrive. The young people can be a bit of a handful as you know. Anyhow, you can rely on my Colin, he won't put up with any monkey business from the youngsters.'

'It sounds like you have it all under control, thank you. What a relief that we decided on the menus well in advance. As you know some of the party will be arriving ahead of schedule, tomorrow, so I'd better let you get on. Keep up the good work, Mrs Armstrong.'

Vivienne went back to the kitchen, feeling pleased, like she'd received a pat on the back.

Later, when she made her way to her own small but charming cottage, she spotted a blue car parked behind their small silver one, on the narrow driveway. Her heart sank when she realised who the owner of the car was.

Two figures were on the doorstep, talking intently, their heads together, Colin and one of the regular chaps from the local hostelry, Tom Barnes, a flinty fellow, who she neither liked nor trusted.

They jumped apart when they heard Vivienne

approaching.

'Hello Vivienne,' shouted Tom. 'Just finished?'

'I have, and your wife and daughter will be finished too, by now. You'd better get a move on,' replied Vivienne, frostily.

'Just on my way,' called Tom, getting into his vehicle and driving off hastily, up the sweeping drive.

'What the heck did he want?' asked Vivienne, suspiciously.

'Nothing, Viv, he was just passing, on his way to collect his wife, and called in to say hello,' replied Colin.

'He never wants "nothing", that one.'

'Stop seeing something that's not there. Come here, woman and give me a kiss.'

Vivienne followed Colin into the cottage, and succumbed to his big bear hug, but was still feeling uneasy at the thought of Tom Barnes having been in her home.

'I just don't trust him, Col,' she said.

A little over a decade ago, soon after Vivienne and Colin had tied the knot, and a few years before they secured their present job, Colin had got in with a bad crowd, and, having been seduced by the dream of big money, was persuaded to get involved with a money-making scam, which resulted in him spending eighteen months at Her Majesty's Pleasure. Vivienne had no idea about any of it, and was truly appalled. They went through a very bad patch, and it was only after he'd been released from prison, having turned over a totally new leaf, that their relationship returned to solid ground. It transpired that being in prison was to be the best thing that could have happened to Colin. He twisted his life around, studied hard, having found he had a passion for gardening and husbandry, so that when they applied for, and succeeded in landing the job at Starlington Hall, they never looked back.

His employers knew about his background, but had been willing to give him a chance. After a short time they realised they'd made the right decision, so impressed were they by his skills, honesty and remorsefulness. Therefore, Colin had a lot to be thankful to them for, and he rewarded both his employers and his wife with an unswerving loyalty.

Tom Barnes had been the one who'd been instrumental in persuading Colin into his short life of crime, therefore, Vivienne was quite within her rights to be wary.

William and Phoebe left London for their drive along the M3 to Hampshire. They had met through mutual chums, at a local yoga class. Phoebe was an interior decorator, full of energy and vim, blessed with a positive, bright personality. She was no slave to fashion, but had chosen today's outfit with extra care. A brown and green dog-toothed check jacket, which had set her back far more than was strictly necessary, brown, tapered corduroy trousers and a bottle green crew necked sweater. The nails on her ring-free fingers were small, clipped and unpolished. Practical hands for her practical job. She wore her naturally blonde hair in a short bob and her only adornment was a gold chain with an astrological charm.

William, his sunny nature deserting him for once, felt anxious at the thought of the weekend ahead. He knew his parents would be hoping he'd met a suitable woman in Phoebe, and even though he'd insisted she was just a friend, which was the truth, he felt certain that his mother in particular might try to read more into the friendship.

'Here we are, Starlington Hall. I always get the jitters,

even after all this time. Silly, I know, but there it is.' William spoke from the heart, turning adroitly into the estate.

'Wow,' said Phoebe. 'What a pile! It must have been some childhood you had here, Will. But why do you say you get the jitters?'

'Oh, I don't know. It's just not my thing, my world. I couldn't wait to escape.'

'It's certainly a million miles away from your current home, that's for sure.'

'Yes. My parents always mean well, and I stopped trying to conform a long time ago, but, well, you'll see,' he replied.

'I'm looking forward to meeting them, and your brother,' Phoebe said, shyly.

Although their relationship was good, relaxed and open, Phoebe had begun to nurse a desire for something beyond friendship, but she kept her feelings to herself. She didn't find it easy to be flirtatious; she was much too practical and sensible to know how to beguile. She'd always found it hard to pick up on any nuance from the opposite sex, which was extremely maddening to her.

Before long the family were sat around the familiar dining table, having a light luncheon of quiche and salad, with new potatoes, followed by an apple crumble and custard.

'My, Mrs Armstrong, this apple crumble is delicious,' remarked William, kindly.

'Thanks, William. I'm glad you're enjoying it.'

The conversation, though stilted to start with, both parents concurrently giving poor Phoebe the third degree, had now settled into one of less tension. Toby seemed pleased to have his brother around to dilute the attention of his parents.

The family had all taken a liking to Phoebe, and were now regaling her with family titbits and incidents from the past, from the boys' childhood, which she found inclusive and heart-warming.

'And what about the time when Toby launched himself head first into the pond, and we all froze, unable to do anything sensible? If it wasn't for Helen pulling him out by his feet, goodness only knows what would have happened,' laughed Duncan.

'Oh that's just great, thanks, folks, I don't remember that,' said an indignant Toby.

'You wouldn't remember, Tobe, you were only about three at the time. Do you recollect it, Will?' put in Philippa.

'Vaguely, yes I think I do. I seem to recall I was more than a little peeved in the aftermath, when Toby was given all sorts of treats, and I wasn't allowed a thing!' said Will.

'That's boys for you, Phoebe. They always seem to think one is being favoured above the other, when in reality they've both always been treated exactly the same,' finished Philippa.

'I'm not sure that's the case at all, Mother, what do you reckon, Bro?' teased William.

Toby smiled, recalling his childhood doubts and insecurities, but aware his mother may have a point.

'All water under the bridge now, at any rate, eh?'

Changing the subject, Duncan turned to Phoebe. 'Do you ride, my dear?'

'I did ride as a teenager, but lost interest after a while. However, I'd love to give it another go, or at least go to see the horses, Lord Duncan.'

'Right, that's settled then. I'll take you down to the

stables to meet the nags. Does anyone else fancy riding out today?' He looked around the table to see if he had any takers.

'I'm afraid I don't have any jodhpurs or riding gear with me,' said Phoebe.

'Oh we can soon remedy that. Come with me, I'll kit you out,' said Philippa. 'We're about the same size. In fact I may well join you both.'

'I think I'll give it a miss today, but I'll definitely ride tomorrow. Would you be kind enough to look after Phoebe, Ma? I want to catch up with Toby,' said Will, pointedly.

'Good idea, come on, Phoebe,' replied Philippa quickly.

They all rose from the table, each feeling contented, happy to have been reunited once again as a family.

Toby and William walked together to the smaller cosy snug at the back of the house, both preferring it to the formal drawing room. Having secured extra coffee from the kitchen, they were just settling in when there was a hesitant knock on the door. Both men called out, 'Come in,' in unison.

Verity came in carrying a tray, which she placed gingerly on the coffee table.

'Thanks. You can leave it with us to do the pouring,' said William.

'If that will be all, sir, thank you.' She made a little bob, not knowing what else to do, and left, feeling a bit self-conscious.

'Pretty little thing,' remarked Toby.

'She is indeed, Bro. But enough of that, now, come on, what's up, Toby?' asked Will, not wanting to beat around the bush. 'What's going on? Why are you here, out of the blue?'

'Oh, Will.' Toby put his head in his hands before looking up into the concerned face of his big brother.

'I don't know what to do or how to tell Ma and Pa. It's complicated. I've got to get it off my chest, or I'll go mad. You see, it's all gone horribly wrong.' Toby took a deep breath, then continued. 'OK, here goes. For some time I'd been suspicious that someone was embezzling funds from the company. It had become very evident, and I felt one hundred per cent certain, but I'd been unable to find any proof. Anyway, I set a trap, and sure enough I found the culprit. It was none other than my charming, self-effacing brother-in-law, Akuchi.'

William gasped, when he realised the implications.

'It gets a lot worse, Bro, you see, I tossed and turned with the knowledge, not knowing what to do, realising the shame it would bring to the family, and especially how much it would impact on Kellan. But I couldn't stand by and watch it happening. So I decided to approach Akuchi, to give him a chance to come clean. He seemed very calm when I accused him, and we spoke about him putting things right without my having to do any whistleblowing. I agreed to give him a week to sort things out, then, before the week was up, I was called up in front of the board, who coolly accused me of the very crime Akuchi was guilty of. When I tried to put my side of the story to them, he was called in. He stood there and lied through his teeth. He said he had proof. He had been busy setting me up to take the rap. All the evidence I'd accumulated had been distorted and altered to well and truly implicate me. He'd done a thorough job, forging my signature on documents, and generally stitching me up. He also had the gall to plead loyalty towards me, as his brother-in-law. He said he'd suspected me all along, but hadn't wanted to shop me. Boy, had I been an idiot.

'When I left the building, a car pulled up and I was dragged inside, taken to the airport and basically put on the next plane to the UK. My dear brother-in-law had collected my passport and some clothes from the house, no doubt feigning a good excuse to Kellan for popping upstairs to grab them. I was told in no uncertain terms, that if I went to the police, Kellan and the children would be in danger. Akuchi and his mobster associates have me by the short and curlies Will, to put it bluntly.'

William leapt out of his chair and held his brother, while Toby broke down in a torrent of grief, which had been held in far too long.

Toby's sobs eventually subsided, but his body was still shaking violently.

'My God, Tobe, I had no idea. We've all been thinking you and Kellan were having problems. I never dreamed it could be anything as horrendous and atrocious as this. Have you spoken to Kellan? Does she know about her brother?'

'That's the worst part, Will. I've tried to call the house and her mobile, but both the numbers have been changed. I can't contact her or tell her the truth. She must be thinking I'm the guilty one, and that I've abandoned her and the children.' At the thought of his wife and twins, Toby's bottom lip started to quiver, and he felt in danger of opening up the flood gates again.

'I'll tell Ma and Pa. That's one burden I can lift from you, but we all need to think hard and work out what to do. I can guarantee one thing for you, Bro, we will sort it out, believe you me. There's got to be a solution, and we'll all be behind you.'

'It's so dangerous, Will, such a corrupt country, and they are sure to have spies here in the UK. In fact I'm pretty sure the house is being watched, so there's no question of us going anywhere near the police. If anything happens to my family I'll never forgive myself.'

'No one will harm your family, Toby, you have my solemn word on that.'

'I feel better for unburdening myself, Bro. I've been going round in circles trying to work out a solution, and I'm at a complete loss.'

The brothers continued to talk for a long time.

All the other guests had started to arrive in good time for dinner that evening, and with such an important weekend ahead for their parents, Toby and William agreed to leave the disclosure of Toby's news until after the weekend.

The dining room was filling up nicely. An array of aperitifs and canapés were being offered by the smart girls and boys in their crisp uniforms of black and white. Introductions were made by the family, who were all well-rehearsed at hosting an event, so that when the guests were finally seated, everyone felt optimistic about the evening ahead.

Nicky was seated next to Dr Antony Vickers and Paula was next to his father, Richard, who was holding forth about tales from the Home Office. Paula learnt that he and Lord Duncan had worked alongside each other for many years, before The Twizzler's retirement. With Richard being the younger man by a few years, he still held a senior post within the government.

Paula was unsure of the protocol when it came to making enquiries into the grand sounding Home Office, as she'd always been led to believe it was top secret government business, and all a bit hush-hush. She did, however, notice that Toby, who had sunk into a brown study, suddenly pricked his ears up when Richard started to recount a tale regarding an incident in Africa. Seemingly he'd had to handle a particularly tricky situation there recently. There were no details given and he was very careful not to divulge any confidential information, and before long he did in fact veer off the subject.

Out of the blue, Richard shot Toby an intense stare.

Paula speculated about what role Richard played, with her mind wandering along the lines of M15 and the like, daydreaming that he was a spy, no less. It was hard to cut in and change the subject. She realised that Richard undeniably liked the sound of his own voice.

'Do stop boring Paula with your tales, Richard,' said his wife, Helen, all of a sudden. 'I'm sure she's heard enough about your escapades for now.'

'Oh, its fine, Helen, thank you, most intriguing,' said Paula, feeling a tad uneasy.

'I know him of old, my dear, if we don't stop him now, he'll carry on all night. Isn't that right, Duncan?'

'That's very true, Helen. Come on old boy, give the ladies a break.'

Everyone laughed, except Toby, who was now looking rather sombre.

'I think it's time to bring up the vintage port, what what? We'll need to lay it down before having a good old guzzle at any rate,' reported Duncan. 'One of you young men needs to pop down to the cellar.'

With that, William, Toby and Antony all jumped up from the table and walked purposefully towards the door.

'Come on, we'll all go down,' said William. The three childhood chums made their way to the stairs leading to the dark, damp, cellar.

CHAPTER SEVEN

Lying in their matching single beds, alongside each other in the vast elaborately decorated bedroom, the following morning, Nicky and Paula, their thoughts still a little muddy and opaque, took in their new surroundings. The bold floral, largely pink and lilac blowsy wallpaper, matching curtains and duvet covers gave them both a sensation of reclining in an overfull, flourishing summer garden.

'Crikey, I almost feel the need of a watering can,' Nicky jested.

Paula laughed. 'I know what you mean, a bit heavy on the hydrangeas, but sooo sumptuous,' she replied sleepily, sliding down, stretching her legs and turning over to snuggle back into her cocoon. 'I'm in no hurry to get out of this bed, it's heaven. What time did they say breakfast was kicking off?'

'Nine thirty I think it was. I'd had so much wine by then…'

'Yes, that was it.' Paula looked at her watch, pulling herself up, reluctantly, to a sitting position, her head heavy and swimming with sleep, 'Oh, we have time, it's only a quarter to eight. Let's have a cup of tea and a gossip.' After a few more groggy minutes, she continued. 'OK, I'll make the tea, then.' Pulling her cover aside and tripping slowly over to the kettle, she busied herself with the task in hand, then brought the two dainty cups and saucers over to the bedside cabinet between the two beds.

Getting back into her nest, plumping the pillows and sitting up enjoying the steaming brew, she was keen to go over the evening with her pal, as they loved to dissect a shared experience.

'What did you think of everyone?'

'Well,' said Nicky, who was just as eager to gossip, 'I really liked Will. He's a bit of a dish all right. I do like a man with curly hair, which is strange considering how I loathe my own unruly mess. And did you notice how Phoebe hung onto his every word?'

'Yes, she's definitely got the hots for him. She seems nice enough. Down to earth, no airs and graces if you know what I mean. She was telling me a bit about her job. She's an interior decorator, which I gather is a bit more than someone who just splashes paint on. She gives out advice on colour schemes, you know the kind of thing, curtains, carpets, blinds and stuff. That must be a bit more interesting than just doing the decorating mustn't it?'

'I'll say, yes. It must make the world of difference. By the way, what about The Waif? Do you see where I was coming from in my description?'

'I certainly do. She's very waif-like, sort of pensive and preoccupied. I quite liked her, even though she's a bit hard to fathom. A chat with her felt a bit like a slow slog through a muddy field! I did feel sorry for her, though. She seemed out of her depth, especially when we all first met, with that dress, which was so wrong, poor thing. It was tricky knowing what to wear, but I think we got it right, doing understated. Mind you, I can't wait to show off our dresses tonight. Get the

Gingham and Velvet label out there!'

'Thank goodness we've got each other for advice. You were right. I felt a bit of a fuddy-duddy in my trim navy get up, but poor Lisa must have felt like a fish out of water in her glitzy number.'

'It's hard to know what the gentry will wear, but I reckon they'll be "all out" tonight at the banquet.'

'Richard and Helen seem nice. They certainly look the part,' observed Nicky. 'They're both very stylish aren't they? I'd say they make a good foursome with Lady Lizbum and Twizzler.'

'Yes, and did you see the look Richard gave Toby?'

'No I can't say I did. I was listening to Antony harping on about the patients at his surgery. He's clearly fallen out of love with being a doctor. I'm glad I'm not one of his patients. I couldn't help noticing that Richard was more attentive towards Lady Lizbum than his wife.'

'I reckon Richard likes his own way you know,' put in Paula. 'He certainly likes the sound of his own voice. I bet he could be quite controlling.'

Paula had a sudden flashback. 'I thought Phoebe and Lisa were both looking bored to be honest. I know that feeling. I used to feel it sometimes when I was with Freddy at one of his gigs, like I was on a different wavelength. I spent scores of nights watching the other wives and girlfriends morphing into teenagers whilst all I wanted to do was go home and get into bed with a bloody good book.'

'Ah well, that was last night. It's a whole new day today! We'd better get on. Do you want to use the bathroom first, Paula?'

'No, you carry on. I'll just have another ten minutes in

my nest!'

The next little while was spent getting showered and dressed. Nicky wore a very smart outfit of pale grey dungarees with a black linen shirt, and Paula, in a change from her normal bohemian style, wore tailored maroon trousers and an up-to-the-minute white top, which had been custom made by Nicky.

Paula sat applying her light make-up, whilst Nicky complained about the extreme amount of curl in her hair, and as ever, Paula was tickled by her attempts to tame it. They both then stood in front of the excessively large mirror, where Paula leaned over to tuck the tag of Nicky's shirt back in, agreeing that they "would do", and proceeded to walk down the long staircase and into the vestibule.

The Twizzler looked very smart in his chosen outfit of plus fours, thick brown socks and rather loud chequered V-neck sweater, as did Richard, Toby and Antony, all in varying shades and patterns. They had all partaken of their first meal of the day, having been served at an earlier time, and were now milling around, eager to start the day's events.

'Good morning, ladies. Don't be put off by this rowdy lot, what what! Do enjoy your day, and we will join you later,' said Lord Duncan, cheerily, starting to usher the men outside.

There was a lot of racket going on beyond the terrace of the enormous Jacobean structure. The dogs had arrived with another crowd of people, the beaters, who had come from the village, where most hailed from, although some would have travelled from further afield. Colin Armstrong was looking extremely well turned out, groomed and fine looking. His thick, wavy shock of coal black hair was slicked back, for once looking under control and neat. He was barking out orders, taking command, and Nicky and Paula were impressed by his organisational skills and fascinated by how precisely he was operating, prompting his new nickname of "Barker".

Horatio and Marmaduke, the chocolate Labs owned by Lord and Lady Soames, were clearly excited by all the activity, growling loudly and ferociously in an effort to show the visiting dogs just whose territory they were on and how important they were.

Dragging themselves away from the exciting events taking place outside, Nicky and Paula made their way into the main dining room.

Vivienne and her extra staff were in the throes of setting up the room for a second breakfast sitting. The two ladies were delighted to see the silver domed serving dishes and platters being put out on to the sideboard. They nudged each other knowingly.

'Breakfast is served,' said Lady Lizbum to the assembled group, after getting the nod from Mrs Armstrong.

William, dressed in jodhpurs and a thick Arran sweater, looked decidedly dashing. Phoebe also had on jodhpurs, borrowed the previous day from Lady Lizbum, which were looking rather more dishevelled and grubbier than Will's pristine ones.

As they started to line up at the sideboard to serve their own breakfast, she turned to Paula, explaining how she'd ridden out yesterday in an outfit borrowed from Lady P, as she had no riding gear with her. She was now apologising for the state of her present clothing, and clearly feeling at a bit of a disadvantage.

'You look quite the part, Phoebe, dear,' intervened Lady Lizbum, who must have ears like a fox, thought Paula.

'Yes, you do Phoebe,' said Paula, kindly. 'I take it you'll be going out riding again today?'

'I am. In fact I could get used to this riding lark. I so enjoyed it yesterday, I think I may take it up again. We had a wonderful hack, although between you and me,' she said, as an aside to Paula, 'I can hardly sit, my bum's that ruddy sore!'

When all the other guests were seated, and Phoebe had sunk gingerly to her chair, Lady Lizbum outlined her choice of plans for the day.

She turned to Nicky and Paula towards the end of her speech, saying, 'I thought we'd leave the fittings until tomorrow morning, ladies.'

'Of course, Lady Philippa, whatever suits you best.'

'Right, then, that's settled. What does everyone want to do?' she enquired placing her hands on her lap and looking, round the table.

There had been suggestions of a walk around the lake, a game of croquet, hacking, or a trip into Romsey in the morning, and a beetle drive and round of whist in the afternoon. Of course, their activities would take second fiddle to the shooting party, and would need to be well controlled. There would need to be an awareness of safety precautions at all times.

There was a pause whilst the guests pondered their options.

Helen was the first one to speak up.

'I would relish a touch of retail therapy, so I'm happy to drive into Romsey.'

'That would suit me fine, too,' said Lisa, quickly.

Paula and Nicky looked at each other and nodded. 'We'd enjoy that. Perhaps we could join you, and all go together?'

'Phoebe and Will are going to be hacking, and I will join them,' said Lady Lizbum, 'so, yes, that's settled. We'll all meet back here for lunch at one, and then you can all decide on your afternoon plans.'

'I'm looking forward to a beetle drive. It'll transport me right back to my childhood,' said Paula, and looking round the table, she noticed some of the women were nodding in agreement.

Upstairs in their room, Paula put on a smart black wool coat and green scarf, and Nicky her quilted black jacket. They both reapplied their chosen lipsticks, and headed downstairs.

'I'll drive,' said Helen, decisively.

The Waif had toned down her outfit today, and looked much more comfortable in smart grey slacks and a good quality trench coat, with Helen sporting a tweed suit. So the four women walked towards a smart large car, and Helen carefully negotiated the driveway, when there was a lull in the shooting.

'I know Romsey well,' Helen informed the party. She drove with confidence, bypassing the town centre and finding the road to Stockbridge which also led to the Waitrose car park. 'I'll park here,' she said, pulling in and parking expertly. 'I can always find something that I want to purchase in the store. Now, shall we stay together, or would it be a better plan if we say we'll meet up later?' she asked. Helen was clearly an organised and decisive woman who was used to being in charge when she had the opportunity. Everyone else in the car was happy to go along with her plan.

All four women were of the same mind, deciding they'd like to go their separate ways. Paula and Nicky wandered along the crowded streets, weaving in and out of the Saturday shoppers. They found an old fashioned petite and elegant department store which they both fell in love with. It stocked so many luxurious, unique wares that their rapturous eyes could hardly take it all in. The two friends both made one or two frivolous purchases which neither needed. And they didn't care. Their mood was blithe, and neither woman wanted to spoil it by being sensible.

They did eventually drag themselves away from the tempting counters. On leaving, Paula made an observation. 'Nicky, I do believe that's the Lone Walker over there,' Paula said, nodding over to a man in a familiar green anorak, just leaving a charity shop. 'It looks like him, and he has the same gait as that chap we saw the other week.'

'So it is. Well spotted.' He seemed to be looking around as if expecting someone. His demeanour was nervous and shifty. He disappeared into a newsagent's shop, and the women carried on with their shopping.

Presently, and walking down the other side of the road on their way to the rendezvous point, Paula and Nicky spotted Helen and Lisa coming out of a gift shop, side by side.

'Ah, you two, coo-ee,' shouted Helen. 'We've just run into each other in the last shop, and now we see you. What good timing,' she laughed. Looking down at her watch, she went on. 'Shall we head back to the car and get going?'

The four women fell in step together and returned to the car park. Climbing into the vehicle they drove along, chatting happily about their outing, their purchases, and what was planned for the rest of the weekend.

Lunch was a fairly sedate affair, with William trying his best to act as host to a table full of women.

Verity Barnes was doing most of the serving, alongside Mrs Armstrong, who was looking a little jaded, having been up since the crack of dawn. She was looking forward to putting her feet up after lunch, in readiness for the long evening ahead. Pleased with the way Verity was working, Vivienne found it hard to believe she was Tom's daughter, her being so polite and helpful.

Verity was finding working at the hall harder than she'd imagined. She'd had to persuade her parents to let her. She was the brightest of all her siblings and Tom and Rosalind were determined to make sure she knuckled down to study for her GCSEs. It was all very well being the teacher's pet and finding lessons easy, but like any other teenager there were things she wanted to be buying which she didn't always want her parents to know about. She was determined to have some level of freedom, and was secretly hoping that if she showed willing it may lead to a permanent weekend position at the hall.

They put the food and drink in the middle of the table and the diners helped themselves to the salad and garlic bread, after being served their plates of vegetarian lasagne.

The main course was followed by a hearty bowl of bread-and-butter pudding with cream.

'Gosh, I'm so full,' remarked Paula, who had enjoyed tucking in. 'Thank you, Mrs Armstrong, you certainly know how to tempt me.'

'It's very nice, I'm sure, to feed someone as likes her

food,' said Vivienne.

'A bit too much sometimes,' said Paula, contritely, tapping her stomach.

'Not at all, Paula,' remarked William. 'It's good to see a woman enjoying her grub, and not holding back. It makes such a change from all those stick insects that continually refuse to eat the merest morsel.'

Phoebe shot a look over to Paula. Will was definitely giving Paula an admiring glance, which wasn't the first one of the day, and unfortunately it was obvious for all to see.

There was a pause and a lull in the conversation.

'We all enjoy Mrs Armstrong's cooking in this house. In fact, let's give her a round of applause,' stated Philippa, who then turned towards her startled housekeeper and began clapping.

Everyone joined in, and Vivienne took a self-conscious bow, which broke the ice, making everyone chuckle.

Back in their floral room, Nicky was teasing Paula about the effect she was having on William.

'I'm not encouraging him honestly. I could have died when he said what he did. And did you see the look I had from Phoebe? I found it really embarrassing.'

'I know you've not been giving him the eye, Paula, you can't help it if you're a vamp!'

'Oh, come on, really. It's not fair. I'm mortified and discomforted.'

'Ooh, mortified and discomforted are you? Get you!'

'Stop it, Nicole flipping Saunders. Come on, we've got the beetle drive in half an hour. Flipping heck, it's all go around here. I do hope they'll not be there, or at least not

William,' Paula tailed off to herself quietly.

CHAPTER EIGHT

Everyone except for The Waif, who was claiming a headache, were now gathered in the drawing room for the beetle drive, which had been set up on old fashioned green felted folding card tables. A pen and paper, ripped from a special pad had been supplied. There was a dice and egg cup in the middle of each table. Paula was transported back to her early days, just as she'd hoped for. She'd been bought up in a guest house where her mother had often run games of this nature. It had always been a beetle drive for the children and whist for the adults.

It hardly seemed possible in the present days of technology, the Internet and smart phones that this kind of pastime had ever even been cooked up! How times have changed, thought Paula.

After Lady P had explained the rules, they played amicably for one round of six. They were having so much fun, that they decided to carry on playing until around four, when Vivienne announced she was about to serve afternoon tea.

Nicky and Paula sat on the settee, where The Waif, whose headache had passed, joined them, and the girls were surprised to find her chattier than at any other time. She was asking them about their business, and seemed genuinely interested in the way they worked and the process of putting together a collection, even requesting more cards to pass around to her friends. She was keen to know how the fitting had gone with Lady Philippa.

'We haven't done the fittings yet. They'll be done tomorrow morning,' explained Nicky.

'Oh, right, I wasn't sure. Are you nervous?' she enquired.

'Well a little,' admitted Paula. 'It's always a bit of a worry that we've got everything right, but we're very particular on that first visit. We have to be.'

'It does sound exciting. So much better than working in an office,' said The Waif with a resigned sigh.

They spoke about Lisa's work at the council offices in Christchurch, which did indeed sound deadly boring. Before long Lady Lizbum called them all together for a few hands of whist.

There were only four takers this time, Phoebe and Will having decided on a walk to the lake, and Lisa (clearly not a games enthusiast) wanting a gander in the library and music room.

Lady Lizbum started to deal the cards.

Through an open window in the drawing room, all of a sudden, came the sound of voices drifting in from the outside.

'Darn this sodding useless thing,' roared a man's thunderous voice. 'It's no use to man nor beast.'

'Hold on, old fellow, I'm not sure it's entirely the gun that's at fault,' declared a second person.

'Well, we'll jolly well see about that,' barked the first voice.

And with that, loud footsteps could be heard moving

swiftly over the terrace and in through the front door, followed by even hastier ones ascending the main staircase.

'Men, eh?' said Helen, having heard the exchange. 'They always make such a fuss. Goodness knows what's going on. If it was a woman, the problem would have been solved by now.'

The other three women muttered a general consensus of agreement.

After a while Paula and Nicky were once again in their floral bedroom, pleased and relieved to be free to rest before having to get ready for the banquet.

'Well I'm glad that's over I must say. I think I feel the need of some fresh air. Are you coming, Nicky?'

'No, I'm staying put. I need a kip before tonight,' replied Nicky, decisively.

'I won't be long and then I'll be doing the same,' finished her friend.

Paula walked down towards the stables and the scattering of outbuildings, noticing that all the shooting seemed to be over for the day, and most of the men were milling about on the vast terrace, drinking tea and boasting about the day's events.

She spotted Phoebe on her own strolling back up the slope towards the side door, not looking particularly happy. There was no sign of William. 'That's strange,' thought Paula. 'I wonder why they didn't stick together for the afternoon.'

Then she saw Barker Colin and Vivienne Armstrong, accompanied by The Waif walking away from the greenhouse together. Lisa was carrying three blooms of orchids carefully, like glass, as if they may break.

'Hello Paula,' said Vivienne. 'We've just been giving Miss Moore a lesson on how to grow orchids. She's very fond of them and Colin is a bit of an expert. We've been choosing some to display tonight, they're something of a favourite with Her Ladyship. I didn't trust my husband in his choice of colour, him being colour blind an all,' she laughed.

'I'm thrilled,' said The Waif. 'My granny, Apple, was obsessed with them, so I grew up thinking they were exotic and rare. I'd no idea I could have a shot at growing them myself.'

She seemed more animated than Paula had ever seen her.

'It sounds like you should seriously consider a career in horticulture, Lisa, you're lit up. Always follow your passion, I say,' said Paula with feeling.

'Here, here,' added Barker Colin. 'That's good advice, that is, lass.'

Paula glanced over at Lisa, whose eyes were shining as she looked down at the outstanding blooms, and felt an unexpected jolt of warmth towards her.

The colour on the walls of her bedroom in the west wing of Starlington Hall perfectly reflected Phoebe's mood, which was decidedly blue. Her suitcase was propped open on the bed, and she alternated between the garments hanging in the wardrobe and the contents left in the case. For someone unused to giving much thought to what she would wear from one day to the next, she'd never encountered so many wardrobe malfunctions. On arrival, she'd felt overdressed in the dog-toothed jacket, then underwhelmed in her rather drab taupe dress of the first evening. But having to wear Lady

Soames' jodhpurs for the second day running, with no suitable top to complement them, just so she could accompany William to the stables had really thrown her off kilter. So to have suffered the humiliation of admiring glances towards the dratted dressmaker from William, was just about the final straw.

Why was it that the harder you tried to gain another person's attention, the less interested they became? Phoebe was not a woman who employed guile or tactics to win men over. She was down to earth and straightforward in her dealings with the opposite sex, but when it came to William, she had begun to feel completely out of her depth.

And to top it off he'd had a phone call whilst they were on their way to the lake which he'd insisted was urgent. So he'd turned round and headed back to the house, with no thought whatsoever for Phoebe, leaving her stranded and feeling very much alone.

She looked at the dress she was about to wear with loathing, but, unable to do anything about her choice, poured herself an extra strong gin and tonic from her secret stash, and sat down miserably at her dressing table to gulp it down.

The four extra men invited to the banquet, after taking part in the shoot, were now relaxing, having changed into their evening wear. All four men looked suitably decked out. They stood in a tight circle and were making a head start on the aperitifs.

The local vicar, Reginald Parry, was droning on about local matters, as was his habit, to an unassuming solicitor, Barry Milton, who was feigning interest, unable to steer the conversation in any other direction. The vicar had a fondness for good malt whisky and had downed his first drink with considerable speed. He now looked around anxiously for a refill. His rather annoying habit of repeatedly clearing his throat was getting on Barry's nerves, whilst his eyes were transfixed by the unpleasant stain on the vicar's dog collar. He idly mulled over what the source of the stain may be. The dapper solicitor kept glancing towards the door, hoping for an addition of more lively company. He was finding it excruciating to put up with these monotonous tones. He made a mental note not to bother attending any of the vicar's church services.

The newest member of Starlington village, Julian Crosby, who had made his fortune in the hospitality industry, with a string of top-notch hotels to his name, interrupted. Determined to curry favour with the hierarchy of the village, he promptly butted in. 'If it's an injection of funds that's needed for the Christmas events you've planned, Vicar, I'm your man,' he said bluntly.

All the other men turned towards the unfortunate Julian, whom they saw as an interloper, wreaking of "new money", with shared feelings of aversion.

'That's a very kind gesture, I'm sure,' said Reginald, begrudgingly.

Julian was dressed in the very latest, up-to-the-minute dress suit. It was in fact brand new, and had cost him a hefty sum. He wanted to look the part. He was tall and lanky with a slight stoop. The businessman's mousy brown hair was slicked back and his moustache expertly trimmed. His blue eyes darted about eagerly. Everything he did was designed to impress the gentry, although sadly in that department he had unfortunately missed his mark. Stinking of new money was the worst crime he could commit amongst the group of men he stood with. The sole purpose of attending the shoot had been to ingratiate him in with the local toffs, and become an elite member of Starlington village. It was all he'd ever wanted. He'd developed a very thick skin remarkably quickly since purchasing his mansion on the outskirts of the village.

'We have a committee already formed,' put in Mike Fisher, a big landowner and local farmer, who had no time for the likes of Julian. 'I'm not sure we need any further input to be perfectly honest, Mr Crosby.'

'Oh do call me Julian, no need to be so formal, now, is there, old boy?'

Mike didn't bother to reply. He walked his heavily built physique boldly over to a waitress carrying a tray of canapés, popped a couple in his mouth and grabbed another drink. It was a definite snub, and one which the pompous Mr Fisher enjoyed immensely.

There was an uncomfortable silence, which was broken by the arrival of Lord Duncan and his sons. They each took a glass from the tray of drinks, and proceeded to take over the general exchange.

'Hello gentlemen, I see you're making yourselves at home, what, what? That's the ticket,' said Lord Duncan, congenially. 'The women shall be along presently,' he said, looking at his watch, and then towards the door.

Richard and Antony Vickers were entering the room. Duncan was struck anew by the similarity between the two. Their features were identical, with their square jaws, strong brows and piercing brown eyes, the only difference being in the hair department. Antony's strong dark hair, which was neatly cut, contrasted markedly with his father's receding

hairline. But that did not detract from Richard's attractiveness. He was very eye-catching. The roomful of men continued their ribbing about the day's events at the shoot, the banter now being back on more familiar ground.

When the ladies started to appear, it felt like a welcome diversion, to a certain extent, the men turning, candidly to appraise each new arrival.

Lady Soames appeared, majestic in her silver lurex gown, matching long gloves and simple jewellery, which was understated yet regal. Helen Vickers looked chic and poised in her dramatic black evening gown, high heeled sandals and carefully chosen accessories. Her expertly dyed golden hair had been fashioned into a magnificent topknot and completed with an ornate hair slide. Phoebe's silk taffeta dinner gown, in petrol blue was modest and elegant. It cleverly emphasised her dark blue eyes, and was a decided improvement on her previous apparel. Lisa, on the other hand, with her frock of oyster pink satin, had the opposite effect. It accentuated her skinny neck by way of a daringly plunged neckline. Her make-up was pale and insipid, leading the onlookers to wonder if she had some kind of eating disorder, or life-threatening disease.

Antony moved to stand at her side, one hand resting in the small of her back.

William complimented Phoebe on her dress, his eyes kind and admiring, resulting in an even deeper crimson to her already gin-infused flushed cheeks, but at least now she was able to conclude that her efforts had finally wielded the effect she'd so desired.

When Paula and Nicky walked into the room, there was a noticeable hush.

Nicky was wearing a classic Grecian styled snow white dress, cut exquisitely, as only she could, and adorned with a narrow gold edging. Her jewellery consisted of a plain gold chain and pearl amulet, with drop pearl earrings. Her powder blue eyes shone out vividly, and the overall effect was one of understated charm. Paula, in stark contrast, wore a poppy-red chiffon dress. It was deceptively simple, low cut with a straight bodice, and floating chiffon panels sewn into the skirt. With her dark colouring, and her hair swept up by a beautiful twinkling comb, she resembled an exotic butterfly.

'Well,' remarked Lord Duncan, with a glint. 'Gentlemen, let me introduce you to the ladies from Gingham and Velvet.'

The men all seemed eager to ingratiate themselves to Nicky and Paula, vying for attention, and trying to impress, so that before long they were surrounded. Both felt a little overwhelmed, ardently wishing they could blend into the background of the elegant drawing room.

The door was opened shortly after that, and Vivienne Armstrong announced in a loud and formal voice, 'Dinner is served.'

The Twizzler sought out Lady Lizbum, saying, 'Come.' He patted his forearm and she slipped her hand through the crook of his elbow, resting her gloved fingers on his black sleeve, and he led her through to the dining room, followed by Richard and Helen Vickers, and the other two couples. Toby led Nicky through, and Paula was almost pounced upon by Julian Crosby. The other men looked on, all seething at being beaten to it, except for the solicitor, Barry Milton, who seemed more taken with one of the waiters.

CHAPTER NINE

The place names had been carefully positioned, interspacing the additional men amongst the family and house guests, and Paula found herself next to William Soames, much to her disquiet, after the wry look she received from Phoebe. She glanced over at Nicky, who was in between Toby Soames and Barry Milton. Sitting to the left of Paula was Antony Vickers.

Paula, aware of wanting to bring both men into the conversation, asked how the families had first met.

'Gosh,' said William. 'I can hardly remember a time when our families weren't linked. Can you, Anton?'

'Not really, no. Let me see, now, correct me if I'm wrong, Will, but as I recall it was my pa and your ma, who met initially, at Oxford. Philippa was something of a blue stocking. It was quite unusual for someone of her class to go up to Oxford in those days, I believe. She had no need, after all.'

'Ma's always been a bit of a maverick, and woe betides anyone who tried to stop her from doing what she wanted! As you've probably gathered, she hasn't changed,' laughed Will.

'When they left Oxford, they drifted apart, and after a few years had both become engaged. They all met up again sometime later, introducing their respective fiancés, and after they all got hitched, the friendship between the four of them blossomed, and the rest, as they say, is history,' finished

Antony.

'We've always wondered if things had been different, who knows, we may have been brothers, eh, Anton, in a manner of speaking?'

Antony ignored the question and promptly changed the subject.

The first two courses had been served, and a fair amount of wine consumed, when Mrs Armstrong arrived at the table carrying a large oval plate with the main dish beautifully dressed and presented. She stood for a few moments and there was a small round of applause. She then departed to carve and serve a number of grouse in the kitchen.

'Let's hope we can replace these birds with plenty more tomorrow, eh, what?' announced Lord Duncan.

'Let's hope not,' said William, under his breath, for only Paula to hear.

He met her eyes and gave her a quick wink.

'Hear, hear,' said Julian, holding up his glass.

Toby had also started to relax with Nicky, and was regaling her with tales from Africa, which she'd become engrossed in. She found him to be a confident and well-informed raconteur. She was even able to bring out his sense of humour, which was no mean feat. She was tempted to probe deeper, to find out his dark secret, but felt it may be a step too far. He was undoubtedly more forthcoming with the more he imbibed and Nicky renewed her original impression of him, realising that he did in fact possess a certain charm.

Helen's attention was focussed on her husband, who was sat a little way down the table from herself. He appeared distracted, and kept losing the drift of the conversation. She was becoming annoyed with the way he was behaving. As a consequence she was being downright rude to her neighbours on either side, by totally disregarding them.

Phoebe had to contend with the droning voice of Reginald Parry, being sandwiched between him and Julian Crosby, feeling extremely hard done by with her designated place. She was becoming more and more wound up. She felt most put out and couldn't understand how she'd not been seated next to William. The pleasure she'd felt at Will's compliment was starting to wane. The vicar was, in Phoebe's opinion being very rude by insisting on drinking whisky with his dinner. He'd obtained a small bottle which he kept by his glass and continued to pour covertly throughout the meal. She found it most offensive.

Julian was turning his attention towards Lisa, who made no effort to disguise her bored expression. She was drinking steadily, casting her gaze around at the other guests, in preference to striking up much of a tête-à-tête with her neighbour. She was finding it a chore to have to listen to Julian. All he seemed to want to do was to boast about how many hotels he had in his chain, how big his mansion was and how many acres he owned.

Julian couldn't wait for the ladies to leave the table when he was hoping the men may loosen up a bit and start to talk about business dealings. He looked over at Richard Vickers and managed to catch his eye, indicating he'd like a private word at some point.

All of a sudden the opening bars of 'Sweet Home Alabama' rang out deafeningly.

Toby jumped up from his place and fished around in his trouser pocket for his mobile device. 'Excuse me,' he said, looking down at his screen. 'I must take this call. It is important,' he announced. He strode swiftly over to the door and exited the room.

Lady Soames' voice could be heard above the rest. 'Really, can't you do without your damned phone for one evening?' she shouted at the retreating figure of her younger son.

Toby was out of earshot by then, but Will reacted on his behalf.

'Mother, it may be an important call he needs to take.'

'Oh I might have known you'd be on his side. Really it's too bad that my two sons have both decided to show their bad manners in one fell swoop.'

The Twizzler decided to step in. 'Enough,' he shouted with authority.

Toby arrived back in the dining room, unaware of the short furore he'd caused.

'Sorry about that everyone. I say,' he said, turning to catch the eye of the man acting as the sommelier, 'could I have a top-up please, my good man?'

Richard Vickers, temporarily jolted from his air of detachment, turned to Philippa and diverted her attention with a joke, and the atmosphere returned to something akin to normality.

It didn't take long, however, before Richard reverted to his former mood. What on earth was bugging him tonight? Philippa was unused to being ignored so pointedly, especially by him of all people. So she turned her attention to the rather bombastic Mike Fisher. Listening to him holding forth was preferable to being openly neglected by the one person she expected to pay her attention.

Mike Fisher was enjoying himself massively. His large

face and bulbous nose, which always showed a deep redness, was now almost purple. He was long-winded in the extreme. And to have the ear of Lady Soames was manna to his soul. He lost no time in painting as evil a picture of the man sat opposite him as he possibly could. Julian Crosby. He seemed to really have it in for him. He knew there may be a dispute coming up soon with regard to some of his land, and he saw this as a good opportunity to get Lady Soames on his side. He ploughed on regardless of the disinterest which the lady was clearly showing. He was a master in self-delusion.

The Twizzler, sitting in his place at the top of the table, seemed content to observe his dinner guests. He was puzzled by his great friend's seeming agitation and wondered at what was troubling him. He was also glad to have quashed his wife's outburst. He continued to keep his thoughts to himself, being satisfied to listen rather than offer much in the way of dialogue. He started to stroke his moustache and drift away into his own secret world.

After all the courses had been served, and the cheese and port were set out in the middle of the table, the ladies partook of a little as was the tradition.

William spoke to Paula, saying he thought it was about time this old-fashioned practice of leaving the men to their port on their own afterwards, came to an end. But his parents would not countenance it, so they all went along with the ritual, in order to uphold the long-held habit.

There was a very lengthy break in proceedings when both the ladies and men left the room. People were milling around in the vestibule to start with and then there were a great many comings and goings. All the guests seemed determinedly focused on finding a spare cloakroom, or nipping out for a quick smoke. Some of the ladies chose to disappear upstairs to use their own rooms to "powder their noses". A number of the party were eager to stretch their legs, so made their way outside onto the vast terrace. Eventually, after an extended break and a further delay to wait for one or two stragglers, order was restored. The ladies then entered the drawing room, whilst the men strode back into the dining room.

As the banquet continued, Verity and her mother Rosalind were consigned to the drawing room to look after the ladies. They provided coffee with after dinner mints, and also offered to serve liqueurs.

Vivienne, who had been joined by Colin, were to facilitate the men, making sure they had enough port, cigars and cheese. The dining room now started to fill up with smoke, the smell of strong cheese, and ribald chat.

Vivienne was well used to these gatherings, and was unfazed by the sort of lewd talk which ensued. She just got on with her job, and took no notice when the men appeared to her to revert back to the schoolroom. The conversation escalated and became louder and coarser the more they had to imbibe. However smutty and vulgar it got, she let it all go over her head and concentrated on supply and demand.

They all continued in this vein, with the stories becoming ever more outrageous, shocking and decidedly boorish.

Out of the blue, Richard Vickers stood up from his place at the table, his chair crashing to the floor dramatically, clutching at his chest, and making sounds like a wild animal in pain. He staggered around the room like someone possessed, knocking into furniture and groaning pitifully. Antony, the first one to react, jumped up, telling everyone to clear a gap, and knelt down on the floor, where his father had now collapsed in a heap. He then shouted at the top of his voice to give him space.

'Pa, Dad, whatever is it? What's wrong?' he asked, undoing his father's top buttons and ripping his bow tie from him. 'Duncan, get someone to fetch my bag. It's up in my room,' he demanded.

Richard was now going into a massive seizure on the floor, jerking sporadically, and foaming at the mouth, unable to get his breath and clearly in terrible pain.

Lord Soames, completely panicked, shouted for Colin to bring down Antony's medical bag, and started to usher all the remaining men into the hallway, where the women, having heard the commotion, had also congregated.

There was pandemonium in the vestibule of Starlington Hall.

'Keep Helen out,' he whispered to William, going back into the room, and shutting the door firmly.

Colin took the stairs at double pace and hastily grabbed Antony's medical bag from his bedroom. After running back down he pushed his way through the crowd, and entered the dining room.

He and Duncan saw in front of them a scene they would not forget in a hurry.

Antony was on his knees, holding on to his father's writhing body, sobbing, saying, 'I need to save him, I need to save him.' He was struggling hopelessly to get him on to his side, so strongly was Richard's seizure attacking him.

'Help me,' pleaded Antony, and Colin and Duncan dropped to their knees, just before Richard went into a final massive spasm.

He went completely rigid in the men's arms, his feral eyes rolling in their sockets, and then abruptly, he finally dropped onto his back, and sprawled limply in front of them.

There he lay, with his wild eyes open wide, and his body lifeless.

Antony checked his pulse, whilst the other men shakily stood up, looking down. Antony shook his head.

'I couldn't save my own father,' he said pathetically. He looked up to the small sea of faces, Lord Duncan, Colin, still clutching the black medical bag, and now his mother, hurrying from the doorway, having broken free from William who had been restraining her with quite a force.

'For the love of God, close his eyes,' whispered Duncan, to Antony.

'Leave her, William,' shouted Antony, standing up and catching his mother, before she dropped to the floor beside her husband.

'Richard,' she wailed. 'Richard.'

She looked at her son, and then to Duncan, Colin and William, who all stood with their heads hung low.

'What has happened to my husband?' she screamed.

Antony guided his mother to the nearest chair, and made her sit. He looked towards Colin, and mouthed the word, 'Brandy.'

Colin dropped the bag to the floor and walked to the drinks' cabinet at the foot of the table. He managed to locate a bottle of the spirit, and along with a clean glass brought it back to the table. He poured out a generous measure and placed it in front of the bewildered woman.

Antony held the glass to his mother's lips and made her drink.

Although bereft, Antony remained temporarily professional.

'Don't move him,' he commanded. 'Duncan, would you telephone for a doctor and the police please?'

Antony had removed his dinner jacket and placed it over his father's upper body.

'No one will be allowed to leave for the time being, until we establish what has happened here,' said Antony, grimly.

Everything seemed to be happening with velocity in the aftermath of the events which took place in the dining room of Starlington Hall that evening, and although it was quite clear to Dr Antony Vickers that his dear father had passed away, this fact would need to be verified by a second doctor before any progression could be made.

The on-call doctor arrived ahead of the police. He spoke at length to Antony, and they both agreed there would need to be an autopsy performed before anyone could pronounce with any certainty what the cause of death was. He would need to await the arrival of the police, to give his professional opinion thus far.

Helen Vickers was becoming hysterical, and would need to be sedated, so when the on-call doctor was satisfied, Antony encouraged his mother away and into her bedroom where they stayed, wishing to be left alone together.

Toby shepherded the remaining guests into the drawing room, and so when the brusque Inspector Simon Kitely, and Sergeant Jennifer Peach, a rather plain woman in her late thirties arrived, they were astonished to find a room full of elegantly dressed individuals, all bewildered and largely inebriated.

The two police officers spoke to the on call doctor, who confirmed that the death needed further investigation. Preliminary indications had led him to suspect a coronary, a stroke or possibly the ingestion of an unknown substance.

On entering the room the police officers were bombarded with countless questions, creating a general scene of mayhem.

After the initial chaos Inspector Kitely proceeded to take charge.

'As you all now know, a sudden death has occurred here tonight, and until we have established the facts, I would ask you all to stay put until we tell you otherwise.'

People were shifting round in their chairs, speaking in hushed tones. Some guests were shocked and upset, whilst others were just plainly irritated at having their evening ruined by this unexpected turn of events.

'Would you please come with me, Your Lordship? Were you in the room when the deceased passed away?'

'Yes I was, and it was most upsetting. He was my oldest and most loyal friend,' Duncan said, his voice faltering.'

'Duncan,' said Lady Philippa, softly. 'Let us both go with the inspector and answer his questions, dear. The sooner we get on with this, the better it will be.' Unused to showing emotion, and battling with herself to adopt a dignified manner, Lady Philippa linked arms with her husband and they both followed the inspector out of the room.

CHAPTER TEN

William and Toby looked bereft watching their parents depart. All of a sudden the consequences of Richard's death seemed to hit home like a bullet.

Mike Fisher jumped up from his place on the sofa and started pacing.

Phoebe reacted quickly by shooting him a look of disdain. 'Would you please sit down, Mr Fisher,' she asked.

'Yes, do,' put in Julian Crosby. 'You're making the ladies nervous.'

'And what would you know about the ladies being nervous?' shot back Mike, instantly.

'Please, gentlemen, show some respect,' said Toby.

William looked around the room, his eyes now resting on the four men who had been at the shoot. 'Gentlemen,' he started. 'Much as we'd like to ask you all to leave here right now, I feel we are duty-bound to accommodate you until we have instructions from the police department. Therefore, I second what my brother has just requested. Respect please, gentlemen.'

Vivienne and Colin, who were also now in the drawing room, after a whispered few words with William rose and offered to make hot drinks for the guests.

Paula jumped up from her chair.

'You look all in, Mrs Armstrong, let me help you.'

Nicky quickly followed her lead, and the four departed to the kitchen.

'That's kind of you both to offer. I must say, it's much appreciated; I really am dead on my feet. Oh dear, what am I saying? With poor Mr Vickers having just…'

'I expect you knew Mr Vickers quite well, didn't you Mrs Armstrong?' asked Paula.

'Yes, we did, didn't we, Colin? He was a frequent visitor to the hall. He was a lovely man, always very civil to us, and ready with a smile and a kind word.'

'Do you think it was his heart?'

'I couldn't say. I've no knowledge of these things. He dropped to the floor and started writhing around. We were all so shocked. Of course, young Mr Vickers started attending to him, but it all happened so swift. Yes it was over with before we knew it. A bad business all round, that's what it was,' said Vivienne grimly. She glanced over at her husband uncertainly, who was now busying himself with the filling of a kettle.

The women encouraged Vivienne to sit at the kitchen table whilst they, aided by the Barker, made several pots of tea, and assembled the crockery etc. on two trays.

'You stay put, Mrs Armstrong. We can manage.'

Nicky and Paula carried the trays through, Colin opening the doors ahead of them as required.

'Everyone helps themselves,' said Nicky, as the trays were deposited on the sideboard.

In the library, where Lord Duncan had guided the police to, Inspector Kitely, who had the distinct look of a chipmunk, was trying to establish the facts.

'Did the deceased have a history of heart problems?'

'Not that I was aware of, Inspector, but I can't be certain,' said Lord Duncan.

'We will need to have a word with his widow, but all in good time. For the present, we need to establish the circumstances leading to Mr Vickers' death.'

'As I've told you, we were all sitting around the table, drinking copious amounts of port, making inroads into the cheeseboard, and chatting. Then, without any warning, as I've already stated, Richard stood up from the table, and the rest you know, Inspector,' Duncan explained, starting to get himself worked up at the endless questioning.

'I know it's laborious, but I need to be thorough. Now,' he went on, turning to Lady Soames, 'you and the ladies were in the drawing room, I understand? When did you know something was amiss?'

'We were talking amongst ourselves when we heard a cry of anguish, followed by the sound of chairs scraping against the floor, and raised voices. We all jumped up and headed out into the vestibule to see what the fuss was about. I wondered if there had been an argument in all honesty,' replied Philippa.

'I take it no one has disturbed or moved anything in the dining room?'

'Not as far as I know. Antony asked for some brandy for his mother, for the shock, you see. Maybe sweet tea would have been more the ticket, I seem to think that's what my mother used to recommend for shock.' Duncan was drifting into a kind of reverie.

'Quite. Well, yes, just one final question for the two of you. Do you know of anyone with a grudge against Richard Vickers?'

'No, we most certainly don't. Richard Vickers didn't have an enemy in the world,' said Lady Philippa sharply.

'I agree wholeheartedly with my wife. Salt of the earth, that's what he was.'

'Thank you for your time and patience. I will come along to the drawing room in due course. Right,' Inspector Kitely finished, 'follow me Sergeant Peach.'

The mood in the drawing room was anything but convivial, and with the effect of the drink now starting to wear off, the four men who had belatedly joined the party were impatient to make tracks home.

'I don't see why we're being held here,' said Mike Fisher, gruffly to Barry Milton. 'What reason would they have?'

'They must suspect something other than natural causes if they won't let us leave,' said the solicitor with authority, raising his voice to let everyone in on his thoughts. He removed his thick black framed glasses and let them dangle between thumb and index finger. He was a quiet and modest man, Barry Milton, but nevertheless he was keen to show off his particular expertise at this point.

Reginald Parry, who was in danger of nodding off, suddenly came to and mumbled something incoherent.

Julian Crosby kept his council and dropped his head down low.

'We know no more than your good selves,' put in William.

Turning towards his brother, he went on. 'Toby, I wonder if Antony has had a chance to call Isobel yet. She'll need to be informed.'

'Who is Isobel?' asked Phoebe.

'She's Richard's daughter, Antony's sister, who lives in France,' replied Will.

'I didn't even know he had a sister,' said a surprised Paula.

'Bit of a black sheep by all accounts. I haven't met her, but Anton says he doesn't have much to do with her,' put in The Waif.

William turned, frowning, thinking it inappropriate of Lisa to comment. 'All the same, she should be informed. I'll pop upstairs. Do you want to accompany me?' asked Will, tersely.

'I could do, yes,' said The Waif, rising from her chair and following William out of the room.

'Well, what a carry on. I'm in need of my bed. Do you think this will take much longer?' commented Phoebe, turning towards Nicky.

Before she could answer, the door to the drawing room swung open, and a hush descended as Inspector Kitely and Sergeant Peach made their entrance.

'Ladies and gentlemen, thank you for your patience. We would like to speak briefly to the four gentlemen who are not staying on these premises tonight. All the rest of you are free to retire for the night, and we will return in the morning to continue our interviews. Thank you, that will be all,' said Inspector Kitely, conclusively. 'So, we'll start with the reverend Reginald Parry.' He looked around to see the vicar rising unsteadily from his seat.

'Well thank goodness for that,' remarked Phoebe. 'I'll be glad to get my head down tonight.' She hesitated. 'No disrespect intended,' she added.

The others joined in with her sentiments, all now ready to retire for the night.

The three remaining men resolved to wait, all now feeling a tad edgy.

Lord and Lady Soames entered the drawing room. They both remained standing near the doorway. 'As I explained earlier, there are two rooms available, but I wonder, under the circumstances if it would be a better plan for you all to retire to your own homes?' asked Lady Soames.

'Here, here,' echoed the dejected bunch of men.

'I was wondering, Your Lordship,' said Julian, jumping up and staring over at Lord Duncan with a sycophantic smile. 'I was wondering about the second day's shoot?'

'That's out of the question, old boy. Couldn't possibly go ahead, out of respect, you understand. We need to postpone it for the time being. I'm sure you all understand?' he looked around the room unflinchingly.

'Oh, yes, Your Lordship, we do indeed,' replied Barry Milton, sincerely.

Mike and Julian made half-hearted grunts of agreement, but were both feeling miffed at missing out on a second day's sport.

'Very well, all, I shall bid you goodnight. It's been a long and eventful day,' said Lord Duncan, finally.

Although Nicky and Paula were unquestionably pooped, they knew that sleep would not come about before they'd spoken.

So, after having washed and changed into their night attire, and made yet another hot drink from their welcome tray, they sat upright in their twin beds, sipping at the hot beverage, and chomping on ginger nuts.

'Well, what a turn of events,' started Paula.

'I know this may sound callous, but I've been wondering about our position now. Will Lady Lizbum and The Twizzler still want to go on the cruise, do you think?'

'That had occurred to me too, Nicky. I mean, we do have a living to make.'

'We have Lady Lizbum's signature on our paperwork, so I suppose we're covered, but I fear it would leave a bitter taste.'

'I know it would, I agree...'

The two chums sat munching their biscuits before Paula continued.

'I mean, changing the subject, that doctor must have a strong suspicion, and if he turns out to be right, well, we have a murderer in our midst!'

'Crikey, Paula, you're right.'

They both went silent, whilst mulling over the implications.

'Richard Vickers seemed a nice man, but to be fair we don't know a lot about him.'

'Do you think he was in a happy marriage?'

'Well, all couples have their off periods, yet they don't go around murdering each other!'

'I know, I know. It was just an observation.'

'For some reason I can't forget about the funny look that passed between Toby and Richard last night. It was during a tale Richard was rambling on about, involving Africa. He did go on a bit, Richard, but Toby suddenly pricked his ears up, and Richard gave him a look I could only describe as... well, sinister, yes, that was it, sinister. And it was odd how he changed the subject. I wish I could remember the gist of it, but I was starting to glaze over at that point.'

'I reckon you've been reading too many detective stories, love.'

'Well it won't hurt for us to keep our eyes open, though.'

'Blimey, Paula, did you pack the gabardine, beret and dark glasses?'

The girls went into a fit of giggles, but when they stopped, Paula said, 'In all seriousness, Nicky, poor Richard is in the morgue right now, and there are a lot of unanswered questions.'

With that, they snuggled down into their crowded summer borders, switched off the lights, and before long had both fallen asleep.

Breakfast was rather a sombre affair, and took place in the family dining room at the back of the house.

Mrs Armstrong looked no more improved than on the previous day, still decidedly gaunt and haggard, so Paula was pleased to see Verity and Rosalind Barnes were still around to help her.

The guests were very subdued, as was to be expected, picking at their food, and not conversing, unable to find a subject appropriate to the situation.

There were noticeable absentees from the table, but Lord Duncan had made a sterling effort, and it was him who eventually spoke.

'As you can imagine, we're all feeling very disheartened by the death of our great friend, Richard, and wish to have some time to come to terms with his passing. I believe the police want to get more statements from you all this morning, but we would be most grateful if, afterwards, you'd be kind enough to wend your way home. I'm sorry to cut short your visit, but in the circumstances... well, I hope you all understand.'

'Of course, Your Lordship,' said Phoebe, graciously. 'I'm sure we all do.'

'Yes, that goes for us all,' agreed Lisa.

'Thank you, my dears. Now, come on, we can't let all this food go to waste. Eat up.'

Everyone felt a bit easier, and helped themselves, as best they could, to eat the remaining food.

There was a ring on the doorbell.

'Oh, I expect that will be the police now,' said Lord Duncan, with a sigh.

'OK, Pa, I'll see to them. You go up to Mother. No need for you to get involved any more. You've both given your statements,' spoke William with authority.

'Thank you, son, I would be grateful not to have to go through it all again.'

Will got up from the table and walked out into the vestibule.

'Good morning, Inspector Kitely,' he said, on finding the same police personnel of the previous day standing inside the hallway. He turned towards the smartly dressed police officer and shook his hand, then nodded at his sidekick, Sergeant Peach.

'We'll use the library for the interviews, Mrs Armstrong. Would you like some coffee or tea?' he enquired, turning to his two visitors.

'Coffee would be very welcome, sir, thank you.'

'I'll bring it along presently,' said Mrs Armstrong.

William showed the law enforcement agents into the

library.

'We may as well start with you,' noted Simon Kitely.

'Well, I don't know what else I can add, Inspector,' said William. 'But yes, OK, fire away.'

The interviews continued, each person giving his or her own account of events. Fingerprints were taken. When all the statements had been laboriously recorded, Inspector Kitely explained that he'd made a note of everyone's address details, so they were now free to go, but may be called upon at any time in the future. Several people had noticed the victim had seemed anxious during the evening of his demise, but apart from that there was no clue as to why he'd passed away.

There was only one remaining statement he must tackle — the widow, Helen Vickers.

He spoke quietly to Antony, who had joined the other guests, explaining his request.

'May I ask do you know when the autopsy will be carried out?'

'Yes, we've requested it be hurried along, and are assured it will be done tomorrow.'

'Well that's a relief at least. I'm very anxious to get to the bottom of this. The symptoms were atypical for a coronary, and indeed a stroke, I agree, but that is the result we're all hoping for. Hard as it is that my father has passed away, I really don't know how we will cope if...' Antony trailed off, unwilling to voice his concerns.

'Indeed, Mr Vickers. Now, if you would be so kind as to fetch your mother, we can get it over with, and leave you in peace.'

Helen made the long and anguished journey down the

staircase and appeared in the hallway, looking strained and pale. Thankfully, Toby had pre-empted the situation by ushering everyone into the drawing room until her interview had been concluded.

'What are your plans, Phoebe? I expect William will want to stay here for a while, won't he?' ventured Nicky.

'Oh I can easily get a train up to town from here,' she replied. 'I've been looking at the timetable on my phone, and they run quite frequently.'

'What about you Lisa?' asked Paula. 'We can give you a lift if you like?'

The Waif looked up from the magazine she was thumbing through. 'Oh, yes, I didn't think of that. You live in Dorset too. Well, if it's no trouble, thank you. I'll have a word with Anton; he is of course definitely planning to stay on.'

'You may want to be with him?'

'He's expecting Isobel to arrive, so no, I would only be in the way. I'd rather get home to be honest.'

'We'd like to have a word with Lady Soames first, so we'll let you know what time we'll be setting off after our meeting.'

'OK, thanks.'

Toby, who had been hovering in the hallway by the library door, heard chairs starting to be scraped back, so he darted back into the drawing room, saying, 'I think they're nearly finished.'

Soon after that they heard the solid front door firmly closing, indicating the departure of the two police officers, followed by the entrance in the drawing room of Lady Soames.

'Ah, ladies,' she said, turning to face Nicky and Paula. 'I'd like a word, if I may?'

Everyone else rose up and excused themselves, eager to get on with the day.

'I've been discussing things with Lord Duncan, and we've decided that we'd like to carry on with our planned trip. After much deliberation we agree it would be a kindness to Helen to honour our arrangement. So I'd like you to continue with the collection. I must say I'll be in no position to immediately succumb to any fittings, but I wondered if you'd be able to return in the middle of next week when we may hopefully be returning to some kind of normality.'

'Very well, Philippa,' said Paula. 'That will give us time to get started on a few more pieces too. We'll need to pop up to your dressing room to collect some items before we depart, if that's all right?'

'Of course, the room's open, just carry on,' agreed Philippa.

With that, the two ladies mounted the stairs once more and entered the dressing room.

'Crikey, I don't remember leaving the room as messy as this. It's just as well we've got a bit of a chance to tidy up. Look, there are threads of cotton all over the carpet. Where did they spring from?'

'I really don't know, but we'd better set to and have a clear up.'

They went round the room, removing what they needed to work on, and putting all the half-finished garments carefully into a spare wardrobe. Then, having unearthed a small vacuum cleaner Paula vacuumed up the messy threads from the carpet.

Whilst looking around Nicky felt puzzled. 'I feel there's something missing in here,' she said.

Turning off the machine, and scanning the room herself, Paula agreed, yet neither of the women could fathom what it was.

'We can't spend any longer in here racking our brains, Nicky. Hey, by the way, I'm super pleased with the decision to carry on with the collection,' she remarked.

They then both scooped up the remaining items and headed back to their bedroom.

After a while there was a timid knock on the door and when it was opened, The Waif was stood outside, looking a bit lost and holding her suitcase in front of her with both hands.

'We won't be much longer, Lisa. Shall we meet you downstairs?'

'Yes, all right, thanks.'

When they were alone again, Paula turned to Nicky and joked. 'Why is it we always end up with the waifs and strays?'

CHAPTER ELEVEN

The rain was lashing down as the three women travelled along the dual carriageway on their way home to Dorset. The conversation had come to a standstill, with no one feeling particularly talkative.

'I'm sorry to have got you into this situation, ladies,' said The Waif, out of the blue.

'There's no need to be sorry, Lisa.   Crikey, no one could have predicted these events. Anyway, Lady Soames still wants us to finish the collection, so all is not lost,' assured Nicky. 'Sorry, that sounds so cold-hearted of me,' she finished, lamely.

'Oh, do they still plan to go away?'

'Yes they do.'

'But wasn't it to be their fortieth wedding celebration? I'd have thought it would have been the last thing Helen would want to do.'

'I guess they know Helen better than any of us, but I do see what you mean…'

'I'm really pleased to be out of it for a while, I must say,' said The Waif, sighing. 'I'm not convinced about this "country" life. It's not for me anyway.'

'How long have you and Antony been together, Lisa?'

'Oh, it's about eight or nine months now.'

'You knew his previous girlfriend didn't you?'

Lisa hesitated. 'Jessica, yes. We were good friends, really good friends... Some people were surprised Antony and I got together, but it was one of those things that just sort of happened. Neither of us planned it,' she concluded, defensively.

'I understand. I expect it's been a bit hard for you at times?'

'Hmm, yes it has. Following on from the "perfect Jessica", who was loved by all has had its moments. In fact, I'm a bit unsure if he's the one for me, to be honest,' she suddenly blurted out.

'Well, I always say, it doesn't have to be forever. If it's not working, well, you just need to move on,' said Paula. 'Mind you, the timing's not ideal for you both right now.'

The Waif felt relieved. She felt a sudden kinship towards her driver, and responded accordingly.

'You are so right. I get really fed up with everyone assuming whenever you meet someone new that you've found "the one". Not everyone wants to find 'the one' for a start,' she said with conviction,

'A girl after our own hearts,' laughed Nicky. 'Hey, we're nearly home. Where do you actually live, Lisa?'

'You could just drop me off near the Somerford roundabout if that's OK?'

'We can take you to your house, Lisa, it's no trouble.'

'No it's fine; I need a couple of things from the shop actually. So perhaps you could pull into the supermarket car park, it's not far from there. That would be great, thanks.'

'OK, will do.'

They continued their journey, both women now feeling wiped out with chatting, and just needing to head home.

'Thank goodness we've got a few hours to come back down to earth before we crack on tomorrow,' said Nicky as they pulled up outside her own home.

After dropping her friend off, Paula remembered she needed milk, so swung onto the tarmac in front of her local corner shop. She also picked up a Sunday paper, eggs, cheese, a loaf of wholemeal bread and, on a whim whilst stood in the queue, a giant bar of dark chocolate. She then headed home for an uncomplicated evening in front of the telly.

Back in Hampshire, Vivienne and Colin were also settling down in front of the television, in need of a night to themselves away from the hall, and its residents. Thankfully the Soames boys had seen fit to dismiss them after supper, kindly deciding they would deal with any further domestic duties.

'What a to-do,' said Vivienne, putting her feet up on the comfy sofa.

'I reckon this is only the start of it all, Viv. If they find there's been any funny stuff going on at that autopsy, them there police are bound to be snooping about. I'll not be happy if they start bringing all that business up again.'

'What do you mean all that business?'

'Well, you know that lot. They'll be looking into everyone's background, and you know what that will mean.'

'But, that's all in the past now, Colin, it's got nothing to do with Richard Vickers.'

'Yes, but, they have a habit of going over old ground. You can bet if someone's got a bit of a past, they'll be under suspicion.'

'Don't be so ridiculous, Colin. You haven't anything to fear. Or have you? What about Tom Barnes? Funny he was here the other day sniffing around.'

'That Richard Vickers had a few secrets of his own, and you mark my words, things could get quite nasty.'

Vivienne sat bolt upright at this revelation. 'What on earth are you talking about? Now come on, out with it, Colin.'

'Hmm, well, I'm going to have to tell you, though you won't like it. I never wanted to get involved, and I'm not, it's just that I know a few things that I'd rather keep to myself. I'd not said owt to you, because I knew you'd only worry,' he said, lighting up a cigarette.

'It started a few years ago. Mr Vickers sought me out in the stables. He'd hinted a bit before, but then he came straight out with it and asked me if I knew of a dealer in the village, who could supply him with drugs.'

Vivienne looked shocked.

'Well, you know, I've tried a bit of weed now and again, on and off, and I suppose he may have smelt it on me, I don't know. Anyway, I didn't see the harm, so I gave him Tom's phone number.'

'I knew he would have something to do with it,' said Vivienne, curtly.

'Well, you knew Tom was a dealer, Vivie... Anyway, I didn't hear any more about it, but the next time I bumped into Tom in the pub, he told me it wasn't just drugs he was after.'

Colin glanced over at Vivienne with an intense gaze.

'What the hell does that mean? What else was he after, Col?'

When Colin revealed the information given to him by

Tom Barnes, Vivienne put her hand over her mouth.

'As I said, I didn't get involved, other than supplying Tom's phone number, it's got nowt to do with me, but now you see the quandary. Do I reveal owt if the police ask me, or keep me mouth shut?'

'I'll have to have a think, Col, but my first instinct is to keep your mouth shut. Let's not put the cart before the horse at this stage, we don't even know what he died of.'

'Anyhow, I'm glad to have got it off me chest to you, Viv, it's been on me mind.'

'This will need careful handling if it turns out Mr Vickers death was suspicious, Colin, it will for sure,' said Vivienne, thoughtfully...

Up at the hall there was a sea of glum faces.

Isobel Vickers would be arriving the following day, and although Helen was looking forward to seeing her daughter, she knew it would be far from easy. Antony had prescribed some tablets which he hoped would take the edge off Helen's anxiety and grief. On top of the shock of seeing Richard die so suddenly in such horrendous circumstances, the thought of his sister, and how she could be, worried him. As with all medication he knew the tablets wouldn't take immediate effect, they'd need a few days to kick in and get into the bloodstream. Seeing Isobel may just tip her over the edge.

Isobel was very highly strung. She'd settled down having got married to a surprisingly placid Frenchman, especially now she had a daughter of her own. He, however, remembered the terrible rows she'd caused, and the way his mother had been affected by them. Friction between father and daughter was the main reason. His mother had been run ragged throughout Isobel's teenage years, acting as the peacemaker. She was three years older than Antony, and he learnt at quite a young age not to antagonise her. Looking back, and now with his knowledge of medical matters, he did wonder if she had a genuine mental health condition, but nothing was ever diagnosed.

Having eaten their supper at an earlier time than usual, towards nine o clock, Toby suggested a snack of cheese and biscuits, as he was feeling peckish.

'Good idea, son,' said his father. 'I'll help you assemble something.'

'Nothing for me, Duncan, I think I'll just go up,' said Helen, weakly.

'Do you want me to accompany you, Helen?' Philippa asked, jumping up.

'No thanks, Pip,' replied Helen. 'I'd just as soon be on my own if you don't mind. You're all being very kind. I'm so very tired.'

Antony left the room to take his mother upstairs, and to sort out her tablets, saying he would return to eat when he'd got her settled.

When they had left, Philippa turned to William, as they were now the only two left in the room.

'I do hope the autopsy is conclusive, and they find poor Richard died of natural causes.'

'Well, we'll find out tomorrow, but I have my doubts, Ma, to be honest.'

'Why do you say that? Whoever would want to see him dead?'

'Search me, Ma, and I don't have much medical knowledge, but the little I do have would sadly not lead me to

123

believe he died of a coronary.'

'I couldn't bear to think he'd been... murdered,' whispered Philippa.

'Don't upset yourself, Ma. Come on, I shouldn't have mentioned it.'

Toby and Duncan came in carrying a tray, with packets of biscuits all half-opened, the cheeses still in their wrappers, assorted plates, knives and butter arranged haphazardly, along with a bunch of shrivelled grapes, a couple of apples and a half-empty jar of onion marmalade, all sticky round the lid.

'Come back Mrs Armstrong, all is forgiven,' joked William, looking at the sorry display.

It did at least cause a smidgen of wit, in the sad snug.

Phoebe had returned to her small flat in the capital and was now completely unpacked, the washing machine humming comfortingly in the background. She was in the habit of unpacking as soon as she returned from a trip, always feeling a need to have her own belongings in their rightful place. She bordered on the edge of obsessive-compulsive disorder when it came to tidiness and orderliness and couldn't stand clutter.

She'd telephoned her parents and her two best friends to tell them about her weekend, and found they were all shocked and intrigued at the events which had taken place. She'd kept the details to a minimum, not wanting to draw any attention to the particular way in which events were unfolding.

She wondered about phoning William, but decided she would curtail, not wanting him to think her too keen, so she pottered about gathering her work paraphernalia together ready for the job she had lined up for the Monday morning. After a few games of solitaire on her laptop, she got herself ready for bed. Happy to be back in her familiar bedroom, she picked up her novel in order to read a few chapters before switching off her bedside lamp.

When Antony had eaten his supper, he decided to retire for the night, so the Soames family were alone for the first time in what felt like a long time.

William looked over at Toby, with a questioning look. He knew what was on Will's mind, and realised this was the opportunity to reveal his situation. He nodded over to Will, who took up the mantle, and proceeded to explain to his parents what had happened in Africa.

Toby allowed his brother to talk without interruption.

'Toby,' said Philippa when William had outlined the sorry tale, 'you poor darling. What a turmoil you must have been in.'

'We need to get onto this straight away, son,' said Duncan, decisively. 'Why ever didn't you tell us before now? Think of the time that's been lost. You surely knew about my position, and how I could make discreet enquiries, Toby?'

'I know, Pa, but you'll have to tread very carefully. I can't stress how dangerous this is. The government in Luanda is as corrupt as hell. That's why I've been reluctant to involve you.'

'But Toby, my boy, the very person who would have been ideal in sorting this out was Richard Vickers, as you surely knew? Alas, it's too late now for that, oh I do wish you'd confided in me. Such a waste of valuable time… Well the first thing we need to establish is that Kellan and the children are safe. I don't understand her not making contact.'

'She'll not have been able to, Pa. That brother of hers has no scruples. He will have filled her mind with lies, and he'll have been relying on my keeping quiet because of my love for her... and the twins...' Toby bit back the tears at the thought of his little family.

'I'll get on to a few people,' said Duncan, standing up and walking towards the door, patting his son's arm on the way out, in a fatherly way. 'Don't worry, son, we'll sort it out.'

'Be careful, Pa, please be careful,' he pleaded.

William followed his father out of the room in a determined manner.

CHAPTER TWELVE

Philippa Soames awoke at dawn of the following day in a stupefied state, in that early morning fog when images at the end of a dream don't entirely disappear, but are drifting along languidly, with nothing making any logical sense. Gradually her mind engaged, and reality set in causing a thud in the pit of her stomach. She closed her eyes again, willing herself to capture the rootless dream, reluctant to face reality.

There was a cup of tea on her bedside cabinet, which looked anything but fresh. She sat up and reached out for it, only to realise she was right in her assumption. It was stone cold.

On peering at her bedside clock, she was horrified to see the time. She'd overslept. Duncan was nowhere to be seen, either in the boudoir or the adjoining bathroom.

Unwilling to climb out of her snug, warm bed, yet knowing there was little choice in the matter, she sighed deeply and began to carry out her morning routine. Eventually she emerged onto the landing in a smart grey trouser suit and pink striped jersey.

Downstairs everyone was gathered in the family dining room.

'Why on earth didn't you wake me, Duncan?' she demanded, on entering the room.

'I thought I'd let you sleep on, dear, you've hardly slept

these last few nights,' replied Duncan.

'We have an important day in front of us, and you know how I abhor lateness.'

William, Toby and Duncan glanced at each other, realising Philippa was back to her prickly self. Her softer side, which she'd shown over the previous day, was at an end.

'How did you sleep, Helen?' she asked, remembering her manners.

'Not well, I'm afraid. Those tablets of Antony's don't seem to be doing the trick, but that's to be expected I suppose.' She trailed off, her mind darting around in a haze.

Philippa noticed Helen was in the same clothes as the previous day, and was looking decidedly dishevelled. Her hair was in a muzz, and her face a blank canvas.

'When breakfast is over, we'll go upstairs and sort you out some clean clothes, Helen.'

'I don't give a damn about clean clothes,'

Antony put a hand over his mother's, gently. 'Philippa is only trying to help, Mother, you may feel better after you've had a nice long soak and some fresh clobber.'

'What's the ruddy point?'

There was a general shuffling at the table. This was not the Helen they knew, but every one of them understood her anger.

Shortly afterwards the two women departed, and the men all felt easier, unused to dealing with displays of emotion at the breakfast table.

'What time do you expect to hear the results of the autopsy, Antony?' Duncan ventured.

'You never can tell, it depends on how pushed they are,'

replied Antony. 'I'm picking Isobel up at three o clock, so I'm hoping the results will be in by then. I can't be away from the surgery for much longer. They've had problems getting me a locum as it is.'

'But surely they have to give you some compassionate leave?'

'Of course, but I don't want to be away for too long.'

'You take as long as you need, Anton my boy, your mother will need your support,' said Duncan. 'It's what your father would have expected, and you know it.'

'Come on, Pa,' put in Will. 'Anton doesn't need any more pressure.'

'I appreciate that, William. I was just saying my bit,' retorted Lord Duncan.

The weight of demands was getting to them all, what with the autopsy result and the situation with Toby, the women's moods, and all being cooped up together for too long, it was little wonder the cracks were starting to appear at Starlington Hall.

Nicky and Paula, on the other hand, back in Dorset, were feeling buoyant and optimistic as they both pulled onto the familiar forecourt.

'How many more designs do we need, Nicky?' asked Paula when they'd entered their premises. 'Shall we have a count up?'

'Hmm, let's see. Most of the evening gowns are done, just the gala one left to do. I've got some ideas for that. We still need two, day dresses, and separates for the day trips, and a few more on board numbers. Where's the list? Ah yes, it's here. I'm hoping the samples have arrived. Have you managed to open the post yet?'

Paula pointed towards her desk which was overflowing with unopened post, by way of a reply.

Nicky looked over to the pile of things they'd bought back from the hall, suddenly feeling overwhelmed by the sheer volume of work they'd have to get through.

Paula could see her partner's eyes darting from one thing to the next, and knew from experience how Nicky could get plagued with stress if she didn't slow down.

'OK,' said Paula, 'you make the coffee, and I'll listen to the answer phone messages, then we'll have a break before we get stuck in for the day.'

Towards the end of the day, Nicky remembered about the autopsy.

'Do you think the autopsy results are in yet? Should we phone, or would that seem inappropriate do you reckon?'

'Inappropriate.'

Just before they left the barn, the telephone rang. Paula answered. 'Oh hello Philippa,' she said. 'Yes, Thursday would suit us fine,' she went on after a longish gap, whilst Lady Lizbum was holding forth at the other end of the phone.

Paula listened to what her client was saying, her face now looking serious.

'I'm so sorry to hear that, Philippa. You must all be devastated.'

Again there was silence, as Paula listened intently.

'Well, if we can be of any help, do let me know. Would it be better if we arrived on Wednesday instead? We could give Mrs Armstrong a hand in the kitchen if she's under the weather.'

After a short gap Paula finished with, 'All right, we'll see you on Wednesday. Take care.'

Nicky, who had been trying to second guess at the exchange could barely wait for Paula to replace the phone in its cradle.

'What's happened?'

'Richard Vickers died as the result of ingesting a monumental dose of arsenic,' she said importantly.

'No,' said Nicky, her hand flying to her mouth.

'The police are treating his death as murder, and may wish to question us all again.'

'Jiminy crickets. We've been in the presence of a murderer.'

'We're going there on Wednesday. Antony and Helen are going home tomorrow, with Isobel, who arrived this afternoon. Seemingly Mrs Armstrong is poorly, so she's only doing a couple of hours a day. I offered to lend a hand if necessary. I felt it was the right thing to do. It's a bit odd, but I feel Lady Lizbum is starting to rely on us.'

'I know what you mean. Underneath all that bravado there seems to be vulnerability. Perhaps she needs some female backup for a change?'

'Yes you could be right. Anyway, I've no real plans for this week apart from missing my yoga class and a vague arrangement, but how about you, Nicky, have you anything planned?'

'I'll miss a rehearsal which won't go down too well, and I'll have to make sure Dad's OK to look after the dog again, but apart from that I'm free.'

'OK, so it's full steam ahead with the collection. I must say, I'm finding it hard to concentrate with all these

unanswered questions rolling around in my head.'

'My head's full of it too. Now I know why the police took our fingerprints, they must have been suspicious from the outset. I wonder when the poison was given, and how? I mean, all the men were in the room, surely it couldn't have happened in full view of everyone?'

'I'm not sure how long it would be after someone's been given arsenic, for it to take effect. Philippa said it was a monumental amount. I'd say it can't have taken long, but I see what you mean about the administering of it. Surely, though, the first thing they'll be looking for is a motive?'

'I still say he and Helen were at odds, but I bet there was more to him than meets the eye.'

'Anyway, Nicky, much as I'd like to carry on surmising, we'll be getting nothing done at this rate. Are you finished or do you want to call it a day?'

'Let's give it another hour.'

Paula was not wholly truthful when she said she had nothing planned for the week. She was expecting a visit from her lover either later on that evening, or the following one. She needed to firm up the arrangement, so when she had the opportunity, she made a quick phone call. They agreed on the following night for their liaison. Although initially disappointed, she resolved to be patient, and submit herself to the thrill of anticipation instead.

When she got home Paula was tempted to Google Richard Vickers, but thought better of it.

So, to take her mind off the whole business in Hampshire, she decided to hang some pictures. She'd been meaning to do this job for a while, but had been putting it off.

Paula, whilst getting on with her work, her social life and things which gave her pleasure, could, by her own admission, be indolent when she wanted to be. Anything which needed a hammer, a nail, or a screwdriver got put aside until the mood was upon her. So she rooted out the pile of prints she had in mind. Some of them were ones done by Freddy which she'd had framed. She loved pictures. Her main problem was finding a space on her walls to house them. So whilst wandering around, wondering where to place them, something struck her. She remembered what was missing from Lady P's dressing room. It was the framed photograph of Lady Philippa wearing her trendy summer coat and Richard Vickers with his Panama hat on, which usually stood on the dressing table next to the full-length mirror.

'Yes that's it. I wonder where that photo went and why it's been removed? Well I never,' she thought.

Nicky arrived home to the customary welcome from Tag. Of course, it was all cupboard love, as all he really wanted, after an initial fuss, was to eat! She got his large bowl off the floor and filled it with a good helping of doggy dinner, which he proceeded to eat as if he'd not been fed for a week, as usual.

She put the radio on and turned up the volume. Hmmm, washing the car or changing her sheets? 'It's a bit cold outside,' she thought. 'I'll do the laundry job instead of standing out there freezing my bits off. That'll have to wait for a while.'

So before giving any thought to her own tummy, and how to fill it, she ran up her stairs, opened her airing cupboard and took out her clean sheets, pillow cases and duvet cover. She soon had the job done, and knew by the time she went to bed it would have slipped her mind so, oh yes, what a self-indulgent surprise it would be when she climbed into her fresh smelling, Egyptian cotton bedding that night. What bliss!

Hence both women had diverted themselves, but as each of them drifted off to sleep, the memories resurfaced. The two friends had a lot to think about, neither one knowing for certain why they felt so caught up in the mystery at Starlington Hall.

They continued to make headway with Lady Lizbum's collection over the following day. Nicky showed the design for the gala dinner gown to Paula. 'Wow, Nicky, fantastic. Shades of Oscar de la Renta, mixed with Madame Gres, a distinct classical flavour. I don't know about you but I've surprised myself at what a kick I've got out of designing for someone of her ilk, and I can see you have to. It's such a change from our usual style.'

'I agree it's been a challenge not to be designing our trendy garb, but what a buzz eh? I liked her silver gown on the night of the banquet, which suited her slim figure, so maybe this one could be in gold, perhaps lurex even? What do you think?'

'Yes, gold would do it, but I'm not so sure about lurex. You're a genius, Nicole Saunders. I wonder if we could suggest the two dresses she wears in Lisbon could be in vintage fabric. Do you think she'd go for that?'

'Why wouldn't she? Her summer coat had a bit of a feeling of a bygone era about it, don't you think?'

'Hmmm, well, I sort of see where you're coming from, but it's actually the opposite. It's probably the trendiest and most modern thing she's got! Let's put it to her, anyway. We'd have to get some great vintage fabric. I'll do some research.'

'It'd be good if she had some more of those Japanese fastenings too, how great would they look on those day dresses?'

'What a fabulous idea. I just love it when our creative juices merge.'

So even though the two women had started out a little frustrated at having to curb their modern design flair, they did now realise that working to a more conventional brief was in fact OK. Both women were feeling excited by their collaboration, and realised the session they'd just had underlined their joint vision for Gingham and Velvet.

Nicky popped in to see Leonard on her way home, and was glad to see he had lost his troubled look. He agreed to look after her energetic dog, Tag, whilst she was away again, in fact he seemed delighted by the idea. She pondered (not for the first time) about buying him a dog of his own for Christmas. He really seemed to enjoy the company of her dearly loved mutt.

So, on Wednesday morning at around ten o' clock, after popping into the barn to water their glossy indoor plants, the two partners took a final look at their plush interior. They'd had the wooden floors stripped and limed and the walls painted in soft buttermilk. There were a few large gilt-framed mirrors and some modern art hanging on the walls and a beautifully upholstered lemon brocade chaise longue positioned in the reception area.

So having departed, they once again found themselves

on the road, armed with large amounts of calico, cotton reels, needles, pins, bias binding, scissors, etc. etc., hopefully well prepared for every eventuality.

'Here comes the Gingham and Velvet roadshow,' laughed Paula, as they sped along the dual carriageway heading in the direction of Hampshire.

CHAPTER THIRTEEN

Vivienne looked out of her cottage window to see a car passing, and felt content in the knowledge that she could now call the day her own. Lady P had been understanding and considerate when she'd explained about her illness. She knew the reason why her diverticulitis had flared up again. It had a lot to do with the stress she'd been under, what with the shoot which had taken a lot out of her and the worry over Colin. Although still very much in love with her husband, she'd come to realise, recently, that part of him would always be restless, and crucially that it was vital for him to have an outlet of some kind. Just as long as that didn't involve another woman, and however much she disapproved of the companionship he sought, she realised she needed to give him space. She had been let down by men in the past, and had vowed to herself never to settle for anything less than complete authenticity. But she also realised that a man like him required a form of escapism. He was a stimulating man to be with. She wasn't bored by him, which was what set him apart from her past lovers, and so what if he liked the odd joint? She did too, on occasions. They had a shared love of hard rock music and fast bikes. She resolved to curb her habit of going off at the deep end each time he said something she disapproved of. She wanted to keep the relationship from going stale and carry on with the excitement. But, now, having learned that there had been a murder committed so close to home, she was afraid. His involvement, however tenuous, made her feel nervous, and she dreaded the police arriving to question them.

The two girls from Gingham and Velvet had offered to help out in the house, which she was thankful for, not only because of her health, but also to keep her distance from the police, who were bound to be snooping around at the hall, so when she'd seen the girls' car passing, she visibly relaxed.

When they arrived at the Hall, Nicky and Paula were greeted by William Soames .

'Ah, ladies, do come in. I'm doubling up as the doorman, as you can see. How am I doing? This is all a bit unexpected, but such a nice diversion, I must say. Ma will be delighted to see you, as am I,' Will stated, looking straight into the eyes of Paula.

Somewhat embarrassed at the welcome, Paula was careful to keep things on a semi-formal basis, by not showing any acknowledgement of his penetrating stare.

'We're hoping to be of some help, seeing as Mrs Armstrong is indisposed. I hope you've all been managing? How are your parents bearing up, William?'

'It's not been a bundle of fun, that's for sure. I expect you've heard the news?'

'About Mr Vickers?' asked Nicky? 'Yes, we were really shocked.'

'Bad business,' said William. 'Helen, Antony and Isobel have gone home, so it's just the four of us. Mrs Armstrong assures us she's sorted out your room, so when you've settled in, do join us in the snug for some coffee and a catch-up. I say,' he said, noticing for the first time the amount of clobber they had with them, 'I'll give you a hand with that lot.'

They all headed up the stairs, William carrying the bulk of luggage destined for the dressing room. The two women went back to their original floral room, shut the door and plonked their suitcases on the floor.

'Well, here we are again,' said Paula.

'Yes, shall we unpack, or do you think we're expected downstairs immediately?'

'Let's head downstairs.'

The family had finished their morning coffee, so when the girls arrived, Will offered to make a fresh pot.

Toby and The Twizzler excused themselves, saying they had some business matters to attend to, and William came back with the coffee and a plate of biscuits.

'Do you want more coffee, Ma?' he asked.

'No thanks, Will. If I have any more, I'll be dancing on the ceiling. You stay with the girls; I'm just going up for a lie down before I drop. We'll do the fittings after lunch, girls. I hope you'll be able to stay for a few days, I really don't know how I'll cope without Mrs Armstrong, but I'm sure we can muddle through together, if it's not too much of an imposition?'

'That's fine, Philippa,' replied Nicky. 'We can crack on with our tacking etc., and then we'll just need to sew and do the finishing in Dorset.'

'How kind you both are. Yes, that does sound like a good plan.'

When his mother had left the room, William said, 'I haven't mentioned it to anyone else yet, but I thought it may be nice for us all to go into Romsey tonight for a meal. Or else I did wonder about trying the Lebanese restaurant in the village, though I'm not sure if Ma and Pa will be keen. They'll probably prefer Romsey.'

'That sounds like a great idea,' agreed Nicky.

'Good, that's settled then. I'm sure it'll do us all good to get out, frankly. We've been cooped up together for too long. It isn't healthy. I need to get back to my boat. I miss the embankment and its zany crowd. I'm so much more at home on my boat. Ma seems to have taken rather a shine to you two, it's unlike her I must say.'

'I think, after what's happened she may feel she needs some female company,' suggested Paula.

'I don't know. Perhaps she misses having a daughter. Toby and I aren't much of a substitute after all.'

'Nonsense, she adores you both. Sometimes we women need more of a chat, that's all.'

'I know, and we men are not great with emotional outbursts. It's the typical British stiff upper lip and all that. Ma was very fond of Richard. In fact, I'm not sure if you cottoned on about that the other night, Paula. It was common knowledge that Richard and Ma had become an item at Oxford, back in the day. It was understood they would get hitched, but then it all fell apart, and eventually along came dear old Pa. It's not a secret, but isn't often referred to in the family. Helen has always felt a bit insecure about it, I think.'

'I did wonder about that, I must confess. But it would have been over long ago?'

'Hmm, well you would hope so, wouldn't you? Anyway, I've said too much already. You seem to have a knack of making me say things I shouldn't, Paula!'

'I was wondering if Nicky and I could have a walk

140

around the famous lake. We heard about it at the weekend but didn't get a chance to see it. We'll be back in plenty of time for lunch. Could you point us in the right direction do you think?'

'Good idea, it's worth a look. You need to walk down past the stables, and then bear to the right, past the Armstrong's cottage, through the gate and along the track, and then you can't miss it. I do have things I need to be getting on with. I'll go and find Pa and Toby, and see you back here at one o' clock. I believe Mrs Armstrong has left some cold cuts in the fridge.'

The girls collected their coats and headed out of the front door.

'Come on, the walk will do us both good,' said Paula. 'So, Richard and Philippa *were* an item at Oxford... Hmm, that's very interesting. I wonder if they were ever tempted to re-visit their affair, after they'd both got married to someone else?' she mused.

'What makes you say that?'

'Oh, you know, a few drinks too many, eyes meeting over a crowded room, a shared memory, a wink! It could have so easily happened... Oh my God, Nicky, do you know what that may mean?' Paula stopped dead in her tracks, turning towards her friend, her eyes wide all of a sudden. 'What if William is Richard's son? It would mean he'd be disinherited. He'd lose a mint. What if he only found out recently and decided to bump Richard off before he blabbed?'

'Really, Paula, William doesn't give two hoots about his fortune. He lives on a canal boat for goodness' sake! Toby's more the materialistic type. Mind you, to be honest, it'd be

Philippa, surely, who wouldn't want the truth to come out. Yes, that's right, it would be Philippa who'd have the most to lose one way or another.'

'Oh look, Nicky, there's Mrs Armstrong, and that must be her cottage. She's waving us over. Come on, Agatha.'

'Hello, you two, where are you off to?' greeted Vivienne, cheerfully.

'We're on our way to the lake. Are we going in the right direction?'

'Yes,' she replied, 'but do come in. Colin's over in the wooded area working. I didn't realise what a long day it would be here on my own. I'd be glad of your company.'

'How are you? Lady P said you're under the weather.'

'Yes I am. It's something I live with, an abdominal condition which flares up now and again. I'm pleased to say I'm having a calmer day today, but I still need to rest.'

'Of course you do. Don't worry about anything at the hall, we're happy to muck in. What a lovely home you have here,' noted Nicky, looking around at the decor.

Vivienne looked pleased. She was proud of her small but homely cottage, and loved to be complimented on it, believing she had a bit of a knack with interior design.

'I love your top, too, it really suits you, Mrs Armstrong,' said Paula.

'Do call me Vivienne, you make me sound ancient, though I doubt there's much difference in our ages. I'm forty-eight by the way.'

'You're right, I'm forty-four and Nicky here is the baby at forty-two.'

'Well then, there you are.'

Vivienne stood up taller and tugged at the striking

mustard hued top in order to show it off better. She brushed her hand back lightly over her brown hair which she wore scraped back from her face in a soft ponytail. There were wispy tendrils escaping from around the sides of her face, softening her appearance. She had pleasant features with unusual greenish eyes, a good skin and a ready smile.

'Paula does Vivienne's top look familiar to you?' asked Nicky, impishly.

'Well, you know I was thinking that. Why?'

'Do you mind if I check the label?'

'Carry on. I got it at a sale in Romsey. It was quite expensive at the full price, but I treated myself when it was reduced.'

'I knew it! Look Paula,' said Nicky triumphantly. 'It's one of ours!'

Paula studied the label sewn on the underside of the top, and sure enough, there was the familiar purple and gold with the discreet emblem "G&V" sewn around it. Gingham and Velvet!

'Well I never did. Are you saying this is one of your garments?' asked Vivienne. 'How did it end up in a shop in Romsey?'

'Tegan,' said the girls, in unison.

'It's my daughter, Vivienne. In the early days, when we were starting out, she would take some of our garments and basically go round to boutiques "hawking" them! We were so short of cash, and had no time for marketing or selling, so Tegan would take a few batches off our hands now and again. Mostly she'd whizz them up to London, where she lives, but I expect she may well have tried other places too. She just used to bring us the precious money when she'd made the

143

sales.'

'What a clever girl, she must have loads of confidence.'

'She does, shed loads, in fact sometimes too much!'

'Well I've noticed the label before, but I didn't connect it to Gingham and Velvet.'

'We wanted something small and discreet. Paula, do you remember how that came about?' asked Nicky.

They both thought back to the summer's evening when they, along with their two daughters, sat around the big stripped pine table in Nicky's shed, halfway through their second pitcher of Pimms, each with a pad of paper and coloured pencils in front of them. They all tried out their individual vision, drawing rough designs, letters, squiggles and different colours. Then there was a sharing of ideas and light-hearted disagreements, until eventually the birth of their smart, distinctive label was born.

They smiled at the memory.

'I think it's fair to say our final label was a joint effort. We had a lot of fun in the making of it. Yes, it's always been like that, we've constantly had our daughters involved in the business. Poppy, that's Nicky's girl, has walked her feet off leaflet dropping around the town, and designing our publicity posters. We're like a little family,' said Paula.

'I rather envy you both that, your daughters, I mean. Colin and I chose not to have any children, though he has a son who lives with his first wife. He's a bit of a challenge to be honest. We've never got on that well, but I bite my tongue, not wanting Colin to think I'm jealous of him.'

'You're in a tricky position. It's never easy as far as I can tell. We both have friends with the same problem. I'm not sure I'd have the patience,' admitted Nicky.

'I knew what I was getting into before I married him, but I did think Tyler would improve as he got older. He's nineteen now, and we're still having problems. Ah well, at least we're happy, and we don't see a lot of him.'

'Does he live locally, Vivienne?'

'Yes, he lives in the village on the small council estate.'

Nicky looked at the clock in the room they were sitting in, noticing it was midday and nearly time for lunch.

'Hey, we'd better be making a move. I don't think we're destined to ever see the famous lake.'

'Here I am, rabbiting on. I was going to offer you a drink, I'm sorry, ladies.'

'We couldn't have fitted another drink in anyway. We'd better scoot now, thanks for our little diversion, it was good to see you and get to know you away from the hall,' finished Paula, getting up from the sofa and walking towards the door, followed by Nicky.

'Do come again,' shouted Vivienne as she waved them off.

CHAPTER FOURTEEN

Unpredictably, Lord Duncan and Lady Philippa decided they would like to try the Lebanese restaurant in the village, with the slightly dubious name of The Beirut Grange. William's idea had gone down well with Toby too, agreeing it would make a welcome change.

The fittings had gone swimmingly, and Lady Lizbum had been bowled over with the designs and fabric samples, congratulating the women on how well they'd imitated her own taste. They'd also challenged her to try new styles and had been impressed at how cleverly they'd captured her essence.

She said she would have no hesitation in recommending them to her circle, although admitted there was a part of her that wanted to keep it a well-hidden secret.

'After all, I don't want anyone else to look better than me,' she'd joked.

So, preparing now for the evening ahead, Nicky and Paula felt jubilant. They dressed in smart jeans and a couple of their own colourful tops, and descended the stairs for a quick aperitif before they all piled into the roomy Range Rover.

When they entered the restaurant, all eyes seemed to be upon their party, some of the clientele aware of whom the family were.

The menu was limited, consisting entirely of Lebanese cuisine, and as a vegetarian, William was in his element, as many of the dishes were meat free. His parents were happy for him to take charge of the ordering, and he chose to start with a mixed meze of baba ghanoush, tabbouleh, falafels, hummus and tahini, followed by a fasolia bean stew for himself and a mix of lamb kofta and fish with garlic and lemon for the rest of the party.

The Twizzler and Lady Lizbum, unused to straying far from tried and tested recipes, were a little apprehensive, but willing to give it all a try, and entered into the spirit of the evening with gusto. It was common for this style of restaurant to be alcohol free, but this one wasn't, so the wine was ordered. It was decided they would leave the car overnight in the village, to pick up the following day, so they could all relax and not have to worry about a designated driver.

The waiters stood in a huddle by the side of the bar, eyeing the latest customers cagily.

'Heavens,' remarked Lady Lizbum, 'I wouldn't want to get on the wrong side of any of that lot. I don't want to appear racist in any way, but they do have a certain presence.'

'I know what you mean.' Laughed Paula. 'Though I must say any one of them would look good modelling designer gear on a catwalk. Take our waiter for instance, he's what you might call devilishly handsome.'

The unfortunate man in question, whilst serving the meze, was scrutinised by the whole party, leaving him feeling perturbed. William, who didn't like to see anyone uneasy, made an effort to reduce his disquiet by asking a few personal questions, and he began to noticeably relax.

Throughout the meal William kept up his banter with the waiter, who was now deferring to Will alone, and did in fact, seem a little enamoured of him. So whilst serving the main course, he bravely asked Will what his name was.

'My name's William Soames,' replied Will.

The waiter stopped in his tracks, dropping the hot dish he was carrying, and backing away from the table, so that his superior came rushing towards their table in order to apologise.

'Soames, at Starlington Hall?' questioned the waiter, dramatically.

'Yes, that's right,' replied a startled Will.

'Where Richard he was stay?' said the man, clearly upset.

'Did you know him?'

'Yes, I know him,' replied the man. 'And someone has gone done him one great harm.' But before he could say more, the man was pounced upon by his superior and one other member of staff, pulling him away from the table and into the kitchen at the back.

The manager walked quickly over to the table.

'Please accept my apologies. Your waiter will be dismissed. Let me introduce you to Husani,' he said, turning to one of the others and clicking his fingers for him to come forwards.

'Husani will be your new waiter, sir, and please enjoy this bottle of fine wine, with our compliments,' he said, turning to the young man. 'Sort it,' he simply instructed, curtly, walking away in a fury.

Everyone at the Soames party table was utterly speechless.

'What the Dickens was that all about?' asked Lord Soames, when he had recovered, scanning everyone's stunned face around the table. 'How on earth could he have known Richard?'

Thankfully the restaurant had started to thin out by then, and there were only two couples left, whom no one recognised, so the disturbance was not viewed by anyone of any consequence, but nevertheless, the remaining diners felt shocked.

'We've never been here before tonight, and I don't remember Helen mentioning they'd tried this place,' said Lady Lizbum, clearly baffled.

'Well, he knew Richard, that's for sure,' said Toby.

'You know,' said Lord Soames, turning to his wife, 'there may be things none of us knew which will start to be uncovered before long. We've not spoken tonight about any of it, and it's been a welcome change to have been diverted. However, there will be plenty of unravelling to be done, as there always is in a murder case. We all need to be ready for a rocky ride, you mark my words.'

Paula and Nicky had remained mute during the exchange, feeling as though they were intruding on family matters, but now Nicky felt forced to make a comment.

'Do you think it would be a good idea if you were to ask for that man's name and contact details, in case the police need to interview him?'

'What a sensible suggestion, Nicky. William, see what you can glean from the manager,' commanded Lord Duncan. 'He may not be willing to play ball. In fact, on second thoughts, leave it with me.'

The Twizzler, now with the bit between his teeth, rose from his place and headed towards the small bar in the corner.

'I don't know if it's wise to get involved,' said Lady Lizbum, nervously.

'It won't do any harm, Ma,' assured Toby. 'We've got to be realistic, as Pa said. There has to be a motive for what happened to Richard.'

'Is everyone full, or have you room for desserts?' enquired Will, changing the subject deftly. 'Come on, Paula, I'm sure you have room for a pudding.'

'No thanks, Will. I'm full up, but I'll have another glass of wine, if there's any left.'

'We'll start on the liqueurs. They usually have a good array in these types of restaurants,' he said, calling for the drinks' menu. They all sat back, drinking the unusual liqueurs which started to arrive at the table with speed, and the conversation returned to other matters.

When the girls got back into the safety of their floral bedroom, and into bed, Paula tentatively sank her head onto the pillow, then after closing her eyes, lifted it again promptly, opening her eyes wide.

'Oh no, I've got the spinning Jenny's,' she moaned. 'I can't remember when that last happened. The bloody room's spinning round and round.'

'And I'll apologise now for my loud snoring. I'm bound to bring the house down after all this drink,' said Nicky.

It was a long night, with several dashes to the loo, a lot of loud snoring and eventually a deep sleep.

When the morning came, both women decided to knock any alcohol on the head for a very long time. Whether they stuck to their plan would remain to be seen, but both were adamant for the foreseeable future.

The rest of the household looked to be in the same state, all nursing hangovers and claiming a lack of hunger.

Strong coffee and toast was the order of the day, and not a lot of dialogue.

Paula and Nicky claimed they needed fresh air before they could make a start on the "tacking", so, standing looking out over the grounds, they said in unison:

'The lake?'

'Ha, the elusive lake,' laughed William.

The two girls wrapped up warm and started their descent downwards, retracing their steps of the previous day.

Whilst the Soames family had been enjoying their Lebanese meal; back at their home in Richmond, Helen, Antony and Isobel were all sitting in the elegant lounge of their neo-Georgian town house, half-heartedly watching a television programme.

Isobel had been on her best behaviour when she'd first arrived in Britain, and had seemed genuinely upset about her father's death. She was supportive and kind towards her mother, and Antony felt relieved to have his sibling there, to share the early days of their mother's grief. She was a petite, slim, dark-haired lady with a direct stare and a sharp mind. She insisted on doing all the shopping and cooking, keen on being able to show off her French culinary skills.

It didn't, however, take long before she reverted to type, and he realised she was still on a short fuse. Little things would annoy her, like the fact that her former bedroom was now used as a general dumping ground. Being short of storage space, Helen and Richard had been glad of the unused room to deposit the overflow of clothes, bric-a-brac, spare bedding and books. There was a perfectly comfortable guest room, but Isobel insisted on sleeping in what she deemed as "her own room". She had cleared some space and made up a bed for herself, but the cluttered room was starting to get on her nerves, and she'd decided to go through the black bags, boxes and odd assortment of baskets and trunks which housed what she termed the "rubbish".

Because of an excess of energy, she didn't appear happy unless she was on the go, so this task had fallen quite naturally to her.

She made piles of "stuff" for the charity shop, sometimes calling out to Helen to check if she was prepared to let a particular item go. Helen was getting more and more agitated, as she felt it was far too early to be making these decisions, but at the same time, was pleased to see Isobel occupied.

'I don't mind letting my things go, Anton, but I dread her asking me about anything belonging to your father. Do you think you could have a discreet word with your sister? Some of these things go back years, and have memories. Really, it's too bad that she doesn't seem to have any thought for my feelings. Why has she always been this way? I often wonder if it's my fault. Your father could always handle her, even if it ended with a row, but I get defeated. I know I'm weak, but I'm only just coping as it is,' said Helen.

Antony reassured Helen, but was nearly at the end of his own tether. He needed to return to Dorset, but the police were reluctant to give them the go ahead to start funeral arrangements. He resolved to telephone Inspector Kitely, and be more assertive, though he did understand the need to keep the body in the morgue. There had been talk of bringing in Scotland Yard, but so far the inspector had stubbornly refused to hand over the case. Antony knew they'd visited his father's office at the Home Office insisting on looking at his father's computer and removing his appointment diary, according to Richard's secretary who had spoken several times to Antony.

He knew his father had been involved with cases which were part of the Official Secrets Act, and since he had never been able to discuss work related problems with Richard, due to the very nature of his position, he felt at a loss.

Maybe it had been a mistake to have decamped to Richmond, but his mother had insisted, and he felt duty-bound to defer to her wishes.

In the still of the night when the hour of darkness was at its blackest, Helen lay awake in the double bed pondering the merits of her late husband. She knew full well the kind of man she'd been married to. Knew of his liking for younger women, and some of the sordid affairs he'd had over the years. His obsession in the early days of their marriage, with Philippa, had passed long ago and she'd born it stoically, forgiving his brief dalliance with the woman who was surprisingly now one of her greatest friends. None of them had ever acknowledged the affair openly. But, of late, she had begun to suspect Richard had met someone special. He had made it clear from the beginning that his job would always take priority, and because of its nature he'd need to be away a great deal. She enjoyed the kudos, and the lifestyle they were able to maintain. There was never a shortage of funds, and not being a clingy woman, it suited her well to have a level of freedom. She chose to overlook his dalliances, finding it preferable not to have to confront the truth in order to uphold her chosen way of life. Her confused mind played over scenes from the past, hushed conversations, hurried comings and goings, faces, suspicions, vague recollections. It was therefore, in a dazed state that she finally fell into a befuddled sleep.

On the following morning Antony decided to telephone Lord Duncan for a chat. Maybe he could shed some light.

Replacing the handset after his call, Antony felt more confused than ever. Duncan was talking in riddles, seemingly more concerned with Toby's dilemma, although he didn't divulge the detail, just that it concerned the company Toby worked for in Luanda, and that it may have involved his father. Then he'd asked him if he knew a waiter who worked at The Beirut Grange, the Lebanese restaurant in the village. This was madness. The exchange hadn't helped in the slightest.

He telephoned Lisa, but she'd sounded distant and closed, leaving him with the feeling that their relationship may have run its course. He had begun to realise this over the weekend of the shoot, and knew it was probably for the best, but had hoped for a friendly ear, if nothing else. So with a sinking feeling, he'd pulled on a pair of walking boots and a warm anorak and let himself out of the front door. He pulled the door shut with a bang and strolled purposefully down the path, not knowing where he was headed but determined to get away. As he turned onto the pavement his step increased until he was walking at a ridiculous pace. He was feeling so pent up and troubled that a phrase he'd heard recently at a medical conference, popped into his thoughts. One day any one of us could leave behind our sanity just as easily as one leaves behind an old umbrella. How true, he thought.

He'd never felt as near to the edge.

Nicky and Paula were surprised and delighted to find the lake, and after walking round its perimeter, discovered a high wall. After locating a partially hidden rusty gate in the wall, they went onto find another patch of garden beyond that. In it were dying flower beds and walking paths, a fruit and nut orchard, fading vegetable plot and racks of beehives. They christened it the forgotten garden.

'Barker Colin has his work cut out all over this estate, it's no wonder they need him to be on a full-time basis,' remarked Nicky as they wound their way back up to the hall. 'Anyway, at least I feel more human now, how about you?'

'Yes, I'm much better. What on earth is that mess up ahead?'

The two friends looked towards the terrace. Just in front were two formal flower beds, cut out with precision. There was not much colour at this time of the year but they didn't expect to see soil spilling out onto the lawn in such a haphazard way.

'It looks like Barker Col is digging a further flower bed, but it doesn't seem to match the other ones, does it? Ah well, I suppose he knows what he's doing,' concluded Nicky.

They continued up the slope and let themselves in through the side door.

CHAPTER FIFTEEN

After receiving the telephone call from Antony, Lisa felt unsettled. She'd been unable to respond in the way she knew he'd been hoping for. Even though she'd tried to come across as the sympathetic girlfriend, she knew she'd missed her mark. What was the point in prolonging something that had lost its source of pleasure? Having had her share of bad relationships in the past, she'd made up her mind to break it off, especially after her conversation with Paula and Nicky, who seemed to understand her point of view. However, after recent events she'd decided to delay telling Antony her decision.

She'd been shocked on seeing the headlines in the daily newspapers, at the amount of coverage the death of Richard Vickers had created, not realising he had been such a prominent figure at the Home Office.

She sat at her laptop now, switching between looking on Ebay trying to find a new coat, and doing some research, which she always found tedious. Maybe she would give the girls from Gingham and Velvet a call. She'd liked their company, and wondered if they may fancy a drink, not knowing they'd returned to Hampshire. She was feeling fickle and restless, undoubtedly due to the phone call.

At the same time, Phoebe was climbing a ladder to put a

second coat of paint on the walls of a lounge in the Tudor house she was working on. She was mulling over the things she'd read in the papers too, as surprised as Lisa was at the amount of detail the press had unearthed. There were photos of the family and a potted history of his life. She'd been inundated with calls from her parents and curious friends who knew of her involvement.

She'd not realised how entwined these two families were, and it seemed an ironic coincidence that she had in fact come across members of both households during the course of her former career. She kept this knowledge strictly to herself.

Of course, William would be tied up, she told herself, that's why she hadn't heard from him since she'd returned to London. I expect he's itching to get back, she thought. When he's back, he'll call.

Back in Hampshire, a few days on, now that the story had broken, the press and the police were constantly around, taking photographs and asking questions, which made it impossible to get back to any kind of routine, and everyone was fed up with it all.

However, Lord Duncan had managed a quick trip to the city, after hastily arranging to meet two of his most trusted ex-colleagues. What they told him, off the record of course, put his mind at rest over Toby and his family, and he was returning home with a gladdened heart.

Will met him at the train station, where he filled him in on the news.

'Thank heavens,' said William.

Toby was pacing the floor when the door opened, but

one look at his father's and brother's faces gave him grounds for optimism.

'Now,' said Lord Soames, when all the members of the family had gathered in the snug, 'I have good news. What I'm about to tell you can go no further than these four walls, is that clear?'

'Get on with it, Duncan, don't be so dramatic,' put in Philippa.

'Well, you know I signed the Official Secrets Act all those years ago, and I took my pledge very seriously, Pip.'

'Now you're being pompous, Duncan,' she retorted.

'For the love of God, will you just tell me, Pa?' demanded Toby.

'You have to understand that whilst I worked at the Home Office in full view of the world, the majority of our operatives do not. They are out in the field, their identity closely guarded from both family and friends. A lot of them have false identities. It's national security we're talking about here. So, I'm unable to go into detail, but I can tell you, Toby, that Kellan and the children are completely safe.'

Toby felt an enormous relief as tears of joy formed in his eyes. 'Thank God, oh thank God.'

'Unfortunately, you, Toby, although you had no idea, and did it with the best of intentions, nearly blew someone's cover catastrophically.'

'What do you mean, blew someone's cover?' he said unsteadily.

'This is where it gets untenable, son, because I can't reveal any more without putting lives in danger. You will just have to take my word for it. In your company, nothing is quite as it seems. The oil industry is a very hot potato, politically, and there's a lot of espionage involved. We need our undercover operatives to gather intelligence, and their methods may at times seem unorthodox. Richard was involved. Yes, he was, and I can assure you he was working towards a resolution. Your family have been under surveillance for a substantial amount of time, with their safety, I must stress, being paramount. Unfortunately he was unable to convey this information you, or indeed to me. I know this would have troubled him. He was to have spoken to me on the very night his life was taken, in fact.' Duncan's voice petered out, a lump having formed in his throat.

'Oh my God, Richard was helping me?' said Toby, in disbelief. 'How the hell was I supposed to know that? I thought…'

'What, what did you think?' put in Will.

'Nothing. Nothing at all, it's just something he said which made me wonder… but, well… what about Akuchi? How does he fit into all this, Pa?'

'As I said, son, nothing is as it appears, I can say no more on the subject. It's closed. We must all be patient from now on. I've revealed more than enough, but as I said at the start, Kellan and the children are safe. That's all you need to know.'

'Toby, you haven't done anything stupid have you?' asked Will.

'No, of course I haven't.' He gave his brother a fierce look, his eyes darkening all of a sudden. It did little to set his older brother's mind at rest.

Turning back to his father, he went on. 'God, I'm so relieved, Pa, thank you. Do you know when I'll be reunited with my family, and return home?'

'No. As I said, and I can't emphasise it enough, it's impossible at this stage to divulge more. We need to sit tight, carry on as if you're taking a prolonged holiday in the UK, and in time we'll have news. Does everyone understand?' he looked round at his family.

'Yes, we understand. What a big relief, Toby,' said Philippa, giving her son a warm hug. She then spoke to her husband. 'I know you can't tell us anything specific, but do you think Richard's death is tied in with this business, Duncan?'

'I have no idea. There's no reason why it should be. Richard was a complex character, Pip, and as I've stated before, we must be prepared for the unexpected. However, it's police business now and we must wait for them to bring about a conclusion. Now, let's continue with our lives as best we can. We mustn't draw any unnecessary attention to Starlington Hall. Right, well I'm off to the stables to take Highwayman for a gallop. Does anyone want to join me?'

'Yes, Pa, I'll come,' replied William.

'Yes, and me, I think a good gallop would be just the thing,' said Toby.

Phillipa declined, saying she'd get on with her crossword.

'Come on then boys. Let's get going. We'll head up to the common.'

Nicky and Paula had settled themselves in Lady Lizbum's dressing room, where the light was good, and had been working away for most of the day. They'd had a snatched lunch of omelette and salad with Lady Lizbum, Will and Toby. The Twizzler had not joined them for luncheon, and no reference was forthcoming as to his whereabouts. So, after clearing away the debris from the table and stacking the dishwasher they had returned to their task, squeezing in another round of successful fittings with Lady Lizbum, just after lunch, and, with most of the garments now tacked, were thinking about finishing up.

'I don't think we need stay any longer after today, do you, Nicky? Let's drive back tomorrow, and be ready to start on Monday at the barn,' suggested Paula.

'I was thinking the very same thing, actually. 'Oh, look, there go the riders. They all seem very proficient, I must say,' remarked Nicky, as she stood by the window watching the three men cantering towards the edge of the estate. 'It must be nice for The Twizzler to be with his two sons, I get the impression they don't get much time together on their own, as a rule.'

'Yes, and isn't it an idyllic setting?' replied Paula, observing how handsome William looked sat astride a big bay. 'I would have loved to have had a pony when I was growing up. I used to drive Mum and Dad crazy about wanting one. Of course it was always just a pipe dream. I understand that now, especially as we lived in a busy town, but you don't think about that when you're ten years old and horse mad. I used to go riding every week.'

'At least you got to do a bit of riding. I had to make do with the banister rail as a pretend horse!'

'Ah, bless! Did you go through the horsey phase too then?'

'Yeah, I think all little girls do, I know Poppy did. That's until she became interested in boys of course. It's funny, the phases we all go through as kids. They all feel like the most important thing in your life at the time.'

'Well right now I'm in my hunger phase! I wonder if Vivienne is back in the kitchen. If not, we may need to rustle something up, though it's the last thing I fancy doing.'

The two women continued to clear away, making neat piles of garments which were ready for their final stages, and all set to transport to Dorset.

Lady Lizbum knocked, and then entered the room before they could call out a reply.

'How are you getting on, ladies?'

'We're finished here now, and were wondering if it's OK with you, whether we should make tracks home tomorrow?'

'Yes, my dears. Mrs Armstrong is back with us full-time now, feeling much better, and my thoughts were along the same lines. I really can't tell you how very much I've appreciated your presence over this last week. You must be in need of cash to buy the fabrics etc, so I have a cheque for you as an interim payment. Of course, you'll be reimbursed for all the time you've spent here too,' she said, pressing an envelope into Paula's hand.

'Thank you very much,' said Paula. 'That will be very useful.'

'Good, that's settled then. I've requested a slap-up dinner tonight for your final evening' she said. 'Shall we say seven thirty?'

'Perfect,' said Paula. 'Thank you.'

When they returned to their room, both Nicky and Paula looked at the cheque inside the envelope, their eyes opening wide at their client's bounteousness.

'Crikey, that's generous. Shall we book a "round the world" tour?' said Nicky.

'Tempting, eh? I must say I reckon we both deserve a holiday.'

Getting ready for their final night at the hall, Nicky insisted on wearing her much loved dungarees, which were quite spectacular, the material a sumptuous array of reds, jades, whites and deep blues, in a design of dragonflies. She wore a simple white long-sleeved top underneath.

Paula, also, decided on her favourite bohemian style, a lime green, swirly patterned maxi dress with a retro look about it, sporting a halter neck and rope belt. Her jewellery was chunky and bold, and she had pulled her hair up into a messy style held up with a patterned scarf of matching vibrant colours.

When they appeared in the dining room, William automatically gave a low wolf whistle. They all laughed, good-naturedly, glad to have Vivienne back at the helm and looking forward to a first-rate dinner.

At the end of the evening Paula and Nicky went along to the kitchen to congratulate Vivienne on her excellent cooking. However, before entering, they heard raised voices coming from within, and Nicky put her hand out to Paula to stop her from entering, which left them both hovering outside.

'I don't care, Colin, you can't go on protecting him like this.'

'But he's my son. I know you never liked that crowd he hung about with, I wasn't keen either for that matter, but he's young and easily influenced. He's learnt his lesson though, Viv. All this business has fair put the wind up him. He'll be steering clear of The Beirut Grange from now on, you mark my words.'

'I know that's what you like to think, Colin, but can we trust him?'

'Believe me, after the way I laid into him, verbally, I may add, he'll not be anywhere near that place again. It's knocked the stuffing out of him. And I hate to say it, but, let's face it, if it wasn't for what happened to Richard Vickers, heaven only knows what trouble he'd have landed himself in.'

'Well I hope you're right, that's all.'

'We've all done things in the past that we'd rather forget as well you know.'

'OK, let's leave it at that. I can't stand here gossiping about this now. I just hope you're right.'

Nicky and Paula looked at each other, wide eyed, like they'd both been slapped by an alien, wondering if they dare enter, and then Nicky knocked on the door.

Vivienne glanced over at Colin with a nervous look, before calling, 'Come in.'

'Ah, hello Vivienne, Colin,' said Nicky, on entering, as if they'd not heard a thing. 'How's it going? I'm glad to know you're back to full health now.'

'Hello you two,' she answered, gingerly. 'Yes I'm much better, thanks. Was the meal to your liking, girls?'

'Wonderful,' answered Paula, taking up the exchange. 'We'll miss your cooking so much. We're off tomorrow, and will have to start catering for ourselves again. I must say cheese on toast and ready meals don't have the same pizzazz, hey, Nicky?'

'No, not at all. But sadly the supermarket beckons from now on. We just wanted to thank you for all the lovely food you've spoilt us with, Vivienne.'

'My pleasure,' said Vivienne, now relaxing.

'I'm not sure if we'll see you again, Colin,' said Paula, reaching out to shake his hand. 'It's been really nice to meet you both. Look after that wife of yours; she's one in a million.'

'Go on with you,' said Vivienne, now laughing.

Colin shook her hand, and then turned to Nicky to do the same. 'Aye, she is that, all right. Cheerio ladies, although I feel sure we'll be seeing you in these parts again one day.'

They'd pulled it off, sure that neither of the Armstrongs suspected they'd been eavesdropping, and so, feeling relieved, they made their way up to the floral room for the last time on this visit.

'What did you make of that?' said Nicky, as soon as they were safely in their room.

'Well, it seems to be connected to the Lebanese lot doesn't it? I was wondering if we could divert to The Beirut Grange on our way home, though I doubt they'll be open on a Sunday morning. We'll be driving that way in any case, so we'll keep our eyes peeled for any mischief afoot.'

'OK, Agatha, let's do that. There's definitely a connection between the staff at The Beirut Grange, Richard Vickers, and now it seems to Barker Colin's son. What was his name, ah yes, Tyler Armstrong. Hmmm I wonder?'

CHAPTER SIXTEEN

The Twizzler had requested that Paula and Nicky pop along after breakfast to his rather austere, masculine · study. He wanted to say goodbye and have a final chat with them on their last morning. Horatio was lying down by his master's big leather chair when they arrived, and Paula, who had bravely overcome her fear of big mutts, was petting him. She'd grown overly fond of the two brown labs, and harboured thoughts of becoming a dog owner. Nicky, who kept a delightful springer spaniel named Tag, whom she loved to bits, felt duty-bound to gently point out to her friend the burden of ownership, and responsibility it involved. She knew her friend well, and suspected she may quickly tire of practicalities after the initial enchantment.

'Duncan, come here,' yelled Lady Lizbum, her voice reaching a crescendo. She was standing shivering in her dressing room half-dressed, having decided on a last-minute change of outfit. 'I can't get this dratted hook and eye fastened. Could you come up here and give me a hand please?'

'Ah, she who must be obeyed is calling,' quipped Lord Duncan. 'Stay there, ladies, I'll just be two ticks… Coming, dear.'

The girls were unsure how to react, but couldn't avoid a snigger.

'Quick,' said Nicky, 'now's our chance.'

'What do you mean?' said Paula.

'Look in his desk I'll look in his jacket pocket,' said Nicky decisively.

'What are we looking for?'

'It's the name and address of the waiter. If he obtained it, it's bound to be in here.'

As if propelled by lightening the two nervy women, unused to searching amongst other people's possessions, and terrified lest he return, set about their search.

'I have it Nicky, but we can't take it. He'll notice it missing. Quick, write it down, oh God, it's not like this in the films. Right, here it is,' she said as Nicky scrabbled around in her bag for a pen, and then retrieved the envelope Lady Lizbum had given them.

Paula read out the address.

'Jaaved Boutros 59, Brookham Road, Romsey.'

'For heaven's sake be quick.'

After what felt like a torturously long time (but was in fact a matter of some seconds) Paula returned the slip of paper to the top drawer of the desk and started to pet the dog again vigorously just in time to hear The Twizzler coming back down the stairs.

They had both turned a light crimson and felt slightly unhinged.

'Ah, there you are. I managed to secure her into the troublesome blouse. You ladies do have to contend with such fiddly items.'

'We do indeed, Lord Soames,' said Nicky briskly.

'How many times do I have to tell you, it's Duncan? I really will have to start insisting,' he said in an unexpectedly furtive manner. hey both gave a forced, weak laugh, because the implied tone of his voice, had led them both to expect him to finish with, 'Or I'll spank you!'

'Now,' he continued, 'I have a little something for you both.' He produced two envelopes from the tray on top of his desk, and gave them one each. 'It's just a little thank you from me and the lads for all the support you've given to us over this period.'

'Oh no, Duncan, Philippa has already settled up very generously, thank you very much.'

'I know she has, but this is from me and my sons. We all appreciate your time, and want to reimburse you accordingly. Call it petrol money if you like. Ha.'

'Well, that's very kind of you, but unnecessary, after all, we've had a wonderful time. Oh, except for the sad business of...'

'I know, my dears, but that's part of it. You see, Lady Philippa would have gone to pieces if you two hadn't been around, I suspect. So there it is. I expect you wish to be off now, we can't impose on you any longer, what, what.'

He rose from his chair and the three walked out into the vestibule, where they were joined by Philippa, Toby and William, who each gave them a peck on the cheek.

'Do come back soon,' said Lady Lizbum.

William, giving Paula's hand a secret squeeze, said to both of them, 'Yes you must. I'm going back to London tomorrow, but do stay in touch. Here's my telephone number,' he said, giving Paula a brightly coloured card promoting the virtues of a street artist.

Toby and his father made similar remarks, and the girls promised to return, and then walked down the terrace steps and onto the forecourt towards their car. Getting in and driving off slowly, they turned to wave at the four figures that were stood in the doorway all waving back.

'That was quite a send-off, hey?' said Nicky, who was the driver on this occasion. 'Look in the envelope, Paula, let's sees what we've got.'

'You mercenary devil, you. I can see your eyes glinting from here. Well… heck, it's £500 a piece, and that's on top of the vast amount of dosh we've already got. By gum, the girl's done good! Oh, don't forget to drive slowly past The Beirut Grange.'

'That was quick thinking on my part, in the study, you have to admit,' said Nicky.

'It could have been a quick exit too. Imagine if he'd come back any sooner. I'm not sure what use it is to us. After all, we can't just knock on his door and start interrogating him.'

They were just approaching The Beirut Grange, and Nicky slowed right down driving as if part of a funeral procession, whilst Paula had a good look. The restaurant was closed, as predicted, with no one of a Middle Eastern persuasion lurking.

'Is it worth stopping to see if there's a name of the proprietor anywhere?'

'I don't think so. What's the address, Paula? Get it out of my bag, it's written on the envelope Lady Lizbum gave us.'

'Drat, I didn't give you the post code. I was so panicked at that stage. There may be a map in the town centre, let's head there.'

'Good thinking, Agatha,' said Nicky, turning towards Romsey.

'This is all a bit mad, yet we're both as bad as each other,' she quipped.

They perused the map and located the road they were looking for, realising that it wasn't far to drive. They were there within five minutes.

'Crikey, it's quite a posh road, but I bet most of these houses have been turned into flats. Look at the size of them. Right, it's on the left-hand side, we're at number 15, so it's a fair way down. Now 33, it's hard to see some of these numbers, OK, 51, start to go a bit slower.

'There it is, number 59, it's the one with all the cars on the driveway. Park a little way down and we'll saunter back on foot. Blimey I wonder how many people live there.'

The two amateur sleuths got out of the vehicle, and tried to look nonchalant as they wandered past the house in question, but there was no sign of anyone in the driveway or anywhere nearby.

They ambled down the road for a while, and then turned to retrace their footsteps, after checking no one was watching them.

As they approached number 59 again, a man with a familiar face had just locked the main front door, and was walking down the driveway. It couldn't have been timed any better.

He turned to walk towards them, and as he did so, recognition struck.

''Ello,' he said. 'I not sure you know me, but I see you. You in restaurant one night, Miss?' he asked.

'Yes we were. Oh, you were the waiter who was serving us, weren't you?' said Nicky, as casually as she could.

'I was, and I wish sorry for way I do,' he replied.

'Oh, that's OK. You had a bit of a shock I think?'

'I did. But should not say that I did say.'

'So, you said you knew Richard Vickers?' asked Paula, innocently.

'Yes. I know. He was good. So good and kind man.'

'Where did you meet him, if you don't mind me asking?' pressed on Nicky.

'At party, I meet with him. I can no talk with you, will be notice. Already at windows they are what you say?'

'Curtains twitching.'

'Yes is right. Tweetching.'

'And you knew Richard well?'

'Yes. But I go now. Already I have lose my job. Please to go. You find kill—'

'Killer?'

'Yes you please to know killer for Richard. I very sad Richard,' he said, dejectedly, and then started walking quickly away from them, with no backward glance.

The girls got into their car and Nicky drove further up the road, did a nifty three-point turn, and drove back down the road the way they'd come. As they passed Jaaved, he shooed them on, making it clear they must not stop. Nicky speeded up, not wanting to cause him more trouble, as he'd shown a look of real fear in his piercing black eyes during their short exchange.

'We're no further forward really, except that we now know he met him at a party.'

'I think we may have to give the Barker or Vivienne a ring over the next few days. They may shed some light if they're willing to talk.'

'Hold on a minute, though, we overheard what they said

171

about the son. How can we suddenly start asking questions without them knowing we were listening at the door?'

'Hmm, it needs some thought. You have to wonder what the police have found out, but we've no way of doing that.'

Detective Inspector Simon Kitely and his sidekick, Sergeant Jennifer Peach, were at that very moment checking the diary of Richard Vickers, noting several entries, which did not tie in with his work schedule. A particular letter had started to feature regularly in the top right-hand corner of the pages, for the last six months. So far, however, they'd drawn a blank as to what the letter meant. Questioning his widow, son, daughter, secretary and even his housekeeper, along with his work colleagues, no one could throw any light on the meaning of the mysterious letter.

They knew if they didn't find a promising lead soon they'd have no choice but to hand over the case to New Scotland Yard. There was some confusion over the exact nature of his role at the Home Office. This led to frustration whilst interviewing his colleagues who all closed ranks and hid behind the Official Secrets Act when rattled. Working on a Sunday went against the grain, but neither wanted to admit defeat.

They'd exhausted the possibilities of family disquiet, or financial problems, but something about the Soames family, and their employees seemed "off". Even after extensive questioning, though, they couldn't put their finger on it, and it rankled.

Monday morning dawned and found Nicky knocking over a glass of water on her bedside table. She'd always wondered why they didn't make bedside cabinets with ridges round the edges. There always seemed to be too much crammed onto hers, a small box of tissues, bedside lamp, a clock, her phone, a book and a glass on a coaster, so she mulled over the idea of ridges as an invention, whilst looking down upon the offending tumbler, now upturned on the floor, soaking the carpet.

'Damn and blast,' she said aloud, pulling back the duvet and padding to the bathroom for a cloth.

She got diverted from her task however, and so after showering, making tea and standing in the kitchen to eat a bowl of cereal, she returned to her bedroom to continue dressing forgetting about the spillage, and promptly soaking her feet anew. 'Damn and blast again.'

Before leaving for the barn she hastily checked her phone for emails. Seeing the familiar name in her inbox, she clicked to open the precious mail from her daughter. Scanning it, excitedly she let out a, "Whoop. She's coming home, she's coming home,' she couldn't help shouting out loud, then, admonishing herself whispered, 'I must stop talking to myself.'

She was in the barn before Paula, which was unusual, so after depositing the milk into the fridge and getting the coffee machine going, she filled the watering can and started to water the plants.

When she heard the key in the door she rushed over to Paula, saying, 'Guess who'll be here for Christmas?'

'I'm guessing it's a certain pretty peach of a girl with long blonde hair!'

'Yeah, 23rd December in the afternoon, she'll be at Heathrow airport. Oh Paula, I'm so happy.'

'I am too, love, very happy for you.' Paula gave Nicky a big hug, and they both danced about in a frantic tribal mix of arm waving, bop and boogie, until they flopped down on the brocade sofa together.

'You've missed her, huh?'

'More than I can say. I must be honest, I wasn't looking forward to Christmas with just Dad and me.'

'We could have a party to celebrate, maybe on Christmas Eve? I expect Tegan will be here by then.'

'Good idea. It'll be something to look forward to. Great.' Nicky poured out two mugs of coffee and Paula produced two chocolate croissants to accompany them, saying she'd skipped breakfast.

'Unlike you to skip your breakfast, Paula,' remarked Nicky, and Paula coloured up slightly thinking of the unexpected visitor she'd entertained before starting her working day.

She couldn't seem to wipe the grin from her face, however hard she tried. It stayed there for several hours, on and off, as she came back down to earth.

CHAPTER SEVENTEEN

Having chosen the fabric for the garments from swatches, approved by Lady Lizbum, the two designers always preferred to collect the lengths of material themselves. They checked every centimetre was perfect before committing to the irrevocability of the sharp dressmakers' scissors. They had planned a trip to London later in the week to complete this pleasurable task. With all the calico slopers now tacked and fitting perfectly, they were looking forward to the final stages of cutting, sewing and finishing the unique collection for their client.

Nicky was also determined to attend the next rehearsal at her am-dram society.

When she entered the hall she saw Antony speaking to Clodagh, the director of the play, quietly, in the corner of the room. He looked over at her and waved. When he could get away he walked determinedly towards Nicky.

'Nicky, I'm so glad to see you,' he said with conviction. 'I know no one knows what to say to me, but if I have to repeat myself once more I swear I'll scream. I've only popped in for a short time to tell Clodagh I can't carry on with the play presently, but everyone is insisting it will help take my mind off things. I know they're all well-meaning but I've had it up to here,' he finished, waving his flat hand back and forth, above his head.

'Shall we escape to the pub, Antony? I'm sure no one would mind under the circumstances.'

'That's the best idea of the day, yes, let's go.'

After a quick word with Clodagh, Nicky and Antony beat a hasty retreat and walked into the nearest watering hole, where she insisted on buying the drinks.

Antony took several long, grateful swigs from his pint, letting out a sigh of contentment. 'Ah, a cold refreshing pint of beer, that's just the ticket. Thanks, Nicky.'

'How are your mother and sister?' Nicky enquired.

'Oh, you know, as well as they can be. The police are being relentless in their investigations, and because we're unable to arrange the funeral, it's as if we're all in limbo. No one can settle until we've had the go ahead. We're all about as spiky as a horse chestnut casing to be honest.'

The conversation, loosened by beer, white wine and relief took a solid, self-propelled direction and they spoke of assorted topics, feeling relaxed in each other's company, enjoying their unexpected jaunt. Antony asked Nicky a lot of questions about herself, really feeling as if he was getting to know her a lot better, and she opened up quite artlessly, surprised at how easily the interchange flowed.

Nicky naturally assumed Antony would have the support of Lisa, but when she mentioned her name, there was a brief silence, as loaded as a suet dumpling.

'I haven't seen Lisa, not since returning to Christchurch. I've telephoned her numerous times, but she's distant and awkward. Between you and me, things haven't been going well for a while now. We both know the writing's on the wall, but neither of us is brave enough to voice it. It's strange in a way, because we got together in the aftermath of a great

176

sadness in my life.' He paused. 'And now here we are with another sadness, and it looks like we'll be parting…'

'You know, Anton, sometimes people come into our lives for a reason, and then go again when the time is right,' said Nicky, gently. 'It's no one's fault, it's just the way it is.'

'How very well put Nicky. I'd not thought of it like that, but that makes a lot of sense,' he said thoughtfully. 'All my friends and family thought we'd got together on the rebound, so to speak. I found myself defending Lisa at every turn because it must have been hard for her to live in the shadow of Jessica. I expect you knew about my fiancée?'

'Yes, I did. You've really been through it over these last couple of years, what with that, and now your father. It's a wonder you're still holding it together.'

'I do wonder myself sometimes. I found it really hard at first, to empathise with my patients, coming to me with their petty niggles. I've questioned whether I'm in the wrong profession on more than one occasion. Maybe I should give it all up and become a deep-sea diver?'

'I see you as more of a circus performer, an acrobat perhaps?' said Nicky, with her head tilted to one side, deciding to inject a touch of humour.

'I have balance issues, so doing a triple somersault is out, I'm afraid, but I've always fancied myself on the dodgem cars. Leather jacket, torn jeans, straggly hair, the sight of drooling local girls and their candy floss, eager but acting cool, waiting for the brooding dark stranger to throw them a look… Ah, yes, that would do it!'

'Blimey, I feel I've unearthed a long-held fantasy,' joked Nicky.

'Hmmm, us men are all the same in the end, eh? Joking

apart, I'm so happy I ran into you tonight, Nicky, you've made me feel almost human again. The strain has been unbearable if I'm honest. The police don't seem to have any idea why my father was murdered. They seem obsessed with some letter that appears in his diary regularly. I'm wondering if they will unearth things none of us need to know. We're imagining affairs, involvement with the underworld, you start to believe anything and everything is possible. I can tell you, it's been hell.'

'Do you think it was anything to do with his job, Antony?'

'The thing is, I don't know how much co-operation they're getting at his office, because if it was connected to a case he was working on, which was delicate, top secret even, would they come clean, and do they have the authority not to?'

'Don't they say the most likely motives for murder are money, love or revenge?'

'That's what I can't figure out. He wasn't tremendously rich, OK, maybe there are... hang on a minute, if that was the case, it must all point towards my poor mother... I've only just given that a thought, money, love and maybe revenge... It's preposterous, I mean, every marriage isn't a bed of roses all the time, I'm sure everyone goes through bad times, and... No, it's preposterous!'

'Of course it is, don't even go down that route, Anton, and wipe it from your mind. 'Gosh,' she said, checking her watch. 'I hate to be a party pooper, but think I'd better get going.'

'Yes, time has flown. Thanks so much again. I've really enjoyed your company. We must do it again, and soon. I'll give you my phone number; do give me a ring, Nicky. I cook up a mean curry, and I'd love you to see my little thatched cottage,' he said looking over to the fire where he could hear the flames licking in the grate.

Nicky took the proffered scrap of paper and got up from her chair, hastily followed by Antony, who insisted on walking her to the car park.

The following day in the barn, Nicky relayed her conversation with Antony to her chum.

'I thought about mentioning Jaaved Boutros to Antony, or The Beirut Grange, but I couldn't bring myself to. Do you think I should have done?'

'I'm not sure, but I reckon I'd have done the same as you. I know what we could do. How about us phoning Vivienne to say we're passing on our way to London tomorrow, and could pop in for a coffee?'

'That's a good shout. Just make it sound casual, and I reckon she'll be pleased we're being friendly.'

'OK. I'll give it a go before we change our minds.'

Paula made the call, and Vivienne was delighted to hear the girls would be calling in. She made a specific time so she'd be able to walk down to her cottage for an extended coffee break.

Although they would need to divert from the London road to Starlington village, it was in the general direction of the capital, so they wouldn't lose much time.

The following day, Vivienne made her way down to her cottage. She'd got ahead of herself up at the hall in order to be able to dash home and snatch a longer break. When she spotted their car pulling into the small driveway, she put the kettle on and went to the door to greet her new friends.

'Hello, you two, how nice it is to see you again so soon. Come in.'

After a general catch-up, both women were aware they didn't have a great deal of time to broach the subject.

'The police and press have been crawling all over the place asking all sorts of questions' said Vivienne, and they both knew this was their opening. It was now or never.

'I'm not sure it's our place, Vivienne,' Paula started, tentatively, 'but, when we went out for a meal to The Beirut Grange the other night, there was a bit of an incident. One of the waiters got quite upset when he knew who we all were, and insisted that he knew Richard Vickers.'

Vivienne shifted in her chair, uncomfortably, so Paula pressed on.

'We were wondering if you knew anything about a party Richard attended, Vivienne?'

'Oh dear, you know about the parties? You see I knew it would all come out in the end, I just knew it. I told Colin it would, although we'd decided he shouldn't mention owt to the police,' she said worriedly.

'Yes, we know there were parties. Why don't you fill us in, Vivienne? It would be a weight off your mind I'm sure. Then we can all put our heads together and decide what to do,' went on Paula, in a soft, encouraging voice.

Vivienne told them all she knew regarding the parties which Richard Vickers had asked Tom to organise a little while after he'd made contact with him over the supply of drugs. He'd also requested an assortment of young men, and girls, to entertain himself and some of his influential cronies from London. It was all supposed to be very low key and private. The parties had all taken place in a hotel not too far from Romsey, deep in the New Forest, and had involved a lot of drugs and debauchery. Most of the partygoers provided by Tom were male staff at The Beirut Grange, and Colin's son, Tyler, unbeknown to Colin until later, had become involved. He'd been working in the kitchen of the restaurant in the evenings, whilst attending college during the daytime. Vivienne insisted he'd cut all ties now, and had nothing more to do with the crowd from The Beirut Grange. There were free drugs and a hefty sum of money given to the young men, which was a big temptation for the likes of Tyler. All Richard's cronies had been clearly very wealthy, travelling down from London in the main, and craving the same pleasure as Richard Vickers. Tyler, she said, had been tempted by the money, and had gone along brazenly for a bit of a laugh, with a couple of his buddies. But he was shocked and scared when he realised what was ultimately expected of him, and was not willing to participate fully. He had a bad time of it in the aftermath of that first party, with threats of violence, and ultimatums. He'd been thought of as naive when he confessed he hadn't understood, and made to feel ill at ease, and stupid.

'He'd had a real scare I can tell you,' said Vivienne. 'Those men can be very intimidating; they stick together and don't put up with any nonsense. But, as I said, Colin sorted it out. Don't ask me any details because I don't know or even want to know. The point is, we've been worried over how much Colin should tell the police. I've been worried sick,' admitted Vivienne.

Nicky and Paula remained silent, digesting the information, trying to assimilate the facts.

'When Richard Vickers approached Tom and obtained the drugs he was after, he befriended Tom, who was an unlikely "mate" if ever there was one for the likes of Richard. It was all a ploy to get to know if he could be trusted, and get him what he wanted, I reckon. Anyway, on one of his later rendezvous he made his request. He put an emphasis on "young good-looking men, who like a good time" apparently. So, well, I must say... putting two and two together...'

'Hang on a minute, Vivienne, are you saying that Richard Vickers was gay?'

'It looks that way to me, yes.'

'I'm speechless,' confessed Nicky.

'I keep wondering if Helen knew about her husband. I've tossed and turned in bed at night mulling it over. Actually, it's a weight off my mind now I've told you, though I'm not sure what Colin will say,' said Vivienne, pensively. Glancing at the clock on the wall, she went on to say, 'I'll have to be getting back to work now, or I'll be missed.'

'Thanks for trusting us,' said Paula. 'We'll have a good think and give you a call this evening. Perhaps you'd better not mention it to Colin yet, for the time being at any rate.'

'OK, I'll hold off until I hear from you. As I said, thanks for listening, and now I really have got to be going. I'm sorry to cut short your visit.'

'We must be getting on, anyway. Thanks for the coffee, and don't worry.'

The girls left, and continued their journey to London, pondering the new facts and talking over the possibilities.

'What a cad that Richard was. Not only with this latest episode, but now I'm beginning to wonder if he and Philippa *did* carry on after they were married, knowing the kind of man he was. Although, well it depends on when he realised he was gay of course. Well, that is unless, oh heck I don't know, I just feel for poor Antony, he doesn't need to know all this detail about his late father. I fear it's going to come out one way or another, though,' said Nicky.

'And Helen, she's going to get a shock, unless she had an idea. You'd have to wonder if she knew what he was up to. Most women would have a suspicion if their husband was up to no good, especially if he was gay.'

'It's looking more and more likely. And I wonder if Jaaved was his lover? I mean he really does seem to be cut up over Richard doesn't he? I wonder if it's his initial that's been appearing in Richard's diary? He could have been meeting him on the quiet. What complicated lives people lead.'

They carried on in this vein until they were on the outskirts of Hammersmith, when full attention was given to the traffic and negotiating the flyover, taking them to the car park they always used, in order for them to hop on and off tubes for the rest of the day.

Driving home feeling tired and weary, but happy to have the fabrics neatly stashed in the boot of the car, they once again turned their attention to Richard Vickers. They decided that Nicky, who was in the passenger seat, would call their new friend as promised and advise her to pass on the details to the police. They couldn't see any way round it, and thought Vivienne would agree, which in the event, she did.

'OK, so that's done. I wonder how Barker will react. He could put up resistance, after all he'll not relish the thought of the police questioning him or his son. I can't imagine him being too impressed. I should think he could have a bit of a short fuse.'

'Yes, I think he has. I hope he's not too angry with Vivienne for telling us. It's more dangerous for him not to tell the police, though. What do they call it, an accessory after the fact or something similar? Obstructing the course of justice?'

'Yes, something along those lines. Anyway, whatever he decides, I have a feeling you may be needed to hold the hand of a certain local GP,' said Paula, thoughtfully.

'Oh no, I'm not falling for that one. I'm not being his "rebound" this time round. I must admit, though, I feel very sorry for him.'

'I know you do, and I do too. He'll need a good friend, that's all I'm saying, Nicky.'

'Yeah, but I know how your mind works. Paulette Fredericks. Getting carried away, thinking it'll turn out to be more than just a new friendship. Payback time for the teasing I gave you over William, no doubt.'

'Ha ha. Touché as they say!'

CHAPTER EIGHTEEN

Paula scissored the cellophane off a bunch of mixed autumnal blooms which had arrived from the florist, and then cut the stems before arranging them haphazardly into a glass vase. She'd read the card and smiled to herself, having already guessed they'd be from Freddy.

She'd had several missed calls over the past couple of weeks, and felt she was neglecting her girlfriends too, who'd also been trying to make contact. She'd felt unable to focus on anything much apart from happenings at Starlington Hall, and realised it was high time she did a bit of socialising.

So, scanning the contacts list on her mobile phone, she made a few calls.

Freddy was quick to respond to her message, and they arranged to meet in a local pub, to have a mid-week meal. He was waiting for her with a glass of Chilean Merlot already placed on a cardboard coaster, and the menu ready for perusal. Freddy, being a minor celebrity in Christchurch always got recognised by a few loyal fans, and so when Paula walked in to join him, all eyes turned toward their table.

'I see you bought your fan club with you, Freddy,' she joked.

'Occupational hazard I'm afraid. Anyway you should be used to it by now,' he replied, sarcastically.

'Of course I'm used to it, just out of practice. Anyway, how are you?' she asked, ignoring the jibe.

'OK, I suppose. I must say, though, I'm getting a bit fed up with it all, the gigs, the touring and recording, it's not got the same appeal it had twenty years ago. I think the time has come for a change.'

'Blimey, I never thought I'd hear you say that.'

'Well, none of us are getting any younger, but the trouble is, it's all I know. It's hard to think of doing a mundane job. Have you any suggestions, Paula?'

'It doesn't have to be mundane; there are plenty of creative endeavours you could start.'

'Oh, yeah, like what?'

'How about managing a new band for instance? Or you could take up your art again. You're a great artist, Freddy. You have a real talent.'

'I do still paint now and again, but it's not a real job is it? Who would want to employ me, anyway, now I'm pushing fifty?'

'Plenty of people would be keen to buy your pictures, I'd have thought, or employ you in something new. Don't be so defeatist, Freddy. Have you looked into it?'

Freddy sighed, looking downhearted, not really wanting to have to face reality. His floppy fair hair was starting to thin, and his features had taken on a craggier look, and Paula realised with an unexpected jolt, that his boyish good looks were starting to wane.

'I think of very little else…'

'Anyway,' he said, suddenly changing the subject, 'where on earth have you been hiding yourself lately? You're becoming harder and harder to track down.'

'Well, you won't believe it but I've got myself involved in a curious situation. Have you read about the murder of Richard Vickers in the papers?'

'Do you mean that chap from the Home Office?'

'Yes, that's right, the very one. Nicky and I were there when it happened. It took place in the home of our latest client. We were there to do some fittings on that same weekend,' went on Paula, warming to her theme.

'Get away! There's never a dull moment for you two, by the sound of it. So… who did it?' asked Freddy, with a hint of light hearted mockery.

'It's starting to get complicated. There are so many angles.'

'Well, it's usually cut and dried isn't it? Most murders fall into one or two categories, when all's said and done. What kind of a chap was he?'

'Jovial sort of a fellow, quite charismatic as a matter of fact, but let's just say he wasn't as he first appeared, and harboured some secrets. There are a myriad of possibilities, that's the trouble.' Paula continued to fill Freddy in on everything that had happened, swearing him to secrecy, just in case he'd be tempted to gossip, although she knew deep down that he could be trusted.

'So, do you think there's any truth to the rumour that the eldest son of Lady Philippa could be his son? Is there a striking resemblance for instance?'

'Not really… Antony, Richard's son, is the spitting image of his deceased father, but the two Soames' men, are, how can I put it — well mixed. I suppose Toby does have a bit of a look of Lord Duncan now I come to think about it. I'd say Will favours his mother though, but it's not always obvious is it?'

Freddy looked thoughtful, mulling over the nuggets of information he'd just gleaned, and, quick as a whippet, decided to inform Paula that he wanted to be "on the case".

Paula berated herself for mentioning any of it to Freddy. Why didn't she learn?

'I'll be up in London next week, staying with Tegan,' he informed her, grimacing at his ex-wife, with a knowing, unspoken look. Their daughter led a fast-paced, chaotic life, but he, like Paula, loved her unreservedly. He was happily resigned to the fact that he'd need to sort any domestic arrangements for the two of them. 'So, I was thinking, as I'll have a bit of time on my hands, I could do a bit of snooping. What do you think?'

'Well, Freddy, I don't know what you think you'll achieve.'

He put his index finger onto his nose and tapped it several times. 'I could find out about those parties for a start. I'm not saying I was ever tempted,' he said, carefully, 'but, let's just say there've been opportunities. I've still got contacts, Paula. You leave it to me, I'll get to the bottom of it.'

How very archetypal of Freddy to think he'd be the one to solve the puzzle.

'Really, Freddy, it's not necessary. I wish I'd not mentioned it now,' she confessed.

'Hey, don't go getting all self-righteous on me, I only said I'd have a bit of a nose around.'

'OK, well let's leave it at that,' she said, not wanting the situation to escalate into an argument.

Both faces now showed a stern countenance, but fortunately their meals were bought over in the nick of time.

Nicky and Paula were concerned about Vivienne. Nicky made a call, in order to find out how Colin had reacted to the news that his wife had confided in the two women.

'Hello Nicky,' she'd said, jadedly, on hearing the question. 'Well, I must confess he wasn't best pleased to start with. He came round in the end though. Anyway, the decision was taken out of his hands when the police turned up at the cottage.

'Apparently, Tom Barnes was found in a ditch, having been set upon by unknown assailants, and left for dead. To cut a long story short he was taken to the local hospital with serious medical injuries and the police were naturally informed, so it wasn't long before they paid him a visit at the hospital. Tom, in his dazed and weakened state, was left with little choice but to give a full confession about his involvement with Richard Vickers. Unfortunately, according to Tom, (who Colin called to see in hospital) was forced to give Colin's name as the first contact. I've never had much time for Tom Barnes, but given his position, I did appreciate he had no alternative. Tom's in a really bad way. According to Colin, he's sorry for dropping him in it. Colin, however, has admitted to both Tom and me that he just feels relieved to have it out in the open. He says the doctors have told Tom he'll be in hospital for a long time before he recovers.

'So, with no choice but to cooperate, Colin has told the police all he knows,' Vivienne concluded.

'Oh dear, you must feel exhausted by it all,' said Nicky.

'I do, but we both feel easier too in a way. Colin's been up to the hall to inform Lord and Lady Soames, so that's a weight off our minds. I just hope we can keep our jobs. The police haven't bought charges against Colin or Tom yet, but we know they won't get off scot-free. But to top it all, you won't believe it, but we've had a bloody break-in at our cottage.'

'No!' said Nicky.

'Yes,' she said. 'We have.'

The weary housekeeper went on to explain how it had come about.

Vivienne had been upstairs cleaning the bathroom on her day off. She started clattering around with her bucket and mop when all of a sudden she heard what sounded like something being knocked over downstairs. She thought it must have been Colin who'd come back unexpectedly, so she called out to him.

With that, she heard footsteps rushing across her lounge floor, followed by the slam of a door.

Without thinking, she rushed down her stairs and nearly tripped over her wooden barrel which housed her collection of umbrellas and decorative walking sticks. This is what must have been knocked over. On looking over to their bureau, she noticed all the drawers were open and had been rifled through. There were papers and stationery scattered all over the carpet and a wholly mess left behind. It fair put the wind up her. After phoning Colin, who thankfully wasn't far away, and checking together for what was missing, the only thing that had vanished was the compact camera belonging to Colin. He'd been taking a few snaps, discreetly over the weekend of the shoot, as requested by Lady P.

They had of course, reported it to the police.

'So you didn't see who'd scarpered then?' asked Nicky.

'No, I wasn't quick enough. By the time I'd reacted and got to the front door there was no one around. I didn't fancy searching outside, but of course, Colin did when he arrived.

There was no sign of anyone though.'

'What a time of it you're having. If you ever want to talk to either of us please don't hesitate to call,' finished Nicky.

'Thanks. That's kind. I'll bear it in mind. How are you both doing anyway?'

'We're fine, thanks, it's you who sounds done in.'

On ending the call, Nicky tried to memorise all the finer points to pass on to Paula, verbatim.

Paula received another call that very evening, which gave the two amateur sleuths further food for thought.

'Hello Paula, it's Will Soames.'

'Ah, William, how are you? Have you settled back into life on the canal?' she asked, wondering how he'd managed to obtain her home telephone number.

'Yes, I'm really glad to be home. I persuaded Ma to part with your phone number, I hope you don't mind? I've been quite busy with the punters wanting caricatures and portraits for their loved ones as Christmas presents; I'm always rushed off my feet at this time of year. It's more than a bit nippy, though, sitting around outside.'

'I do a mean line in knitted scarves, you know. I've always got one on the go. I find it relaxing, when I can find the time, that is. I could see you in a Dr Who number.'

'I may take you up on that, Dr Who mode, hmm, classy... I could do with a new one though.'

'How is Phoebe, Will?'

William hesitated, perplexed by her enquiry.

'I'm not sure. I've not been back to my yoga class yet, but I expect I'll see her there next week,' replied William, lightly.

Paula felt a change of subject may be opportune.

'And is Toby still at home, or has he gone back to Africa now?' she enquired.

'Oh, Tobe will be in the UK for a while longer yet. He's unable to return to Luanda for the foreseeable future, Paula,' William replied, a grave quality creeping in.

'I see. Do you think his wife may be joining him at any point?' she asked. 'After all, he must miss his family I'd have thought.'

'He does, very much. I can't give you full details, Paula, but there's a situation in Africa which is very delicate indeed, and Toby must continue to lie low for the time being.'

'Oh that's a shame... I was wondering if he'd managed to speak to Richard on that first night, after dinner.' Paula knew she was skating on thin ice mentioning this, but ploughed on, trying hard to feign an innocent facade.

There was a long silence, whilst William digested her words.

'Oh I wouldn't set too much store by what Richard said. He always liked to imply he knew more than he was letting on. I think it was all part of his persona, he'd been the same when we were growing up, keen for us boys to imagine he led a life of intrigue and adventure. He was well known in the family for it. I'm sure there was nothing sinister to it, Paula.'

There was that word again.

'Actually, now you come to mention it, I think Helen reprimanded him for sounding off... well, as long as Toby's OK, that's the main thing.'

'As I've said to you before, Paula, you have a habit of making me say things I shouldn't, you wicked woman.'

'Ha, ha, moi? Really? How can you say that, Will? You know I'm just an innocent bystander,' Paula whispered coyly. She knew she'd overstepped the mark, and was patently aware that now she'd started to sound outlandishly flirtatious. A change of subject was paramount.

'So, how is the book coming along, and what is the genre you write in, Will?'

'What a butterfly mind you have, Paula, I can't keep up with you. OK, so let's see, in answer to your first question, I haven't done any serious writing for a while. I need to be completely in the moment to concentrate. I did read through the last couple of chapters, but alas, inspiration didn't come, so I've left it alone for the time being. And your subsequent question is answered more easily. I write spiritual books with a universal wisdom, I think, at any rate I like to hope, I'm getting across a message of sorts.'

Paula hesitated before replying, 'Are you aspiring to be the next Paulo Coelho or Eckhart Tolle?'

'Ah, yes, if only, Paula. No, I don't have big aspirations, and am not looking for huge success, but I'd love to think my books may touch the heart.'

Paula felt herself unexpectedly warming towards this multifaceted man, and felt a pull in his direction, realising they had much more in common than she'd known, and feeling momentarily confused with her emotions. She took a deep breath before replying, 'It sounds fascinating, Will, and I'd love to chat for longer, but I'm afraid I have things to do. It was good talking to you, but for now, I must say au revoir.'

'I hope you mean that,' said Will, quietly. 'I'm glad it's au revoir. That's a start.'

CHAPTER NINETEEN

Reluctant as they were to give up on their investigations into the murder of Richard Vickers, Inspector Kitely and Sergeant Peach realised their time on the case was at an end. They had been given orders to hand the case over to New Scotland Yard, so were sitting on the train heading towards the capital for a debriefing session. There was little banter between the two officers, who both felt deflated and downhearted. In the aftermath of the confession given to them by Tom Barnes, they had come down hard on Colin Armstrong, questioning him at length, along with his son, Tyler. There would be consequences to their behaviour, but that would be addressed at a later date. The one extremely interesting fact they'd unearthed, after further enquiries, was that the hotel in which the infamous parties took place belonged to Julian Crosby, who had attended the banquet at Starlington Hall on the night in question.

Mr Crosby had been given a thorough grilling by the detectives, but denied any connection to the murder victim. He also stated that he didn't get involved with the day-to-day running of any of his hotels. As far as he was concerned no irregularities had come to his attention.

The unfortunate manager of the hotel in the New Forest was hauled over the coals by his boss. He insisted that there were no complaints to report on any of the nights Richard

Vickers had booked the suite of rooms which included the penthouse. Plus, every demand for payment had been settled promptly. The regular arrangement proved very lucrative to the hotel, in fact, insisted the manager.

The hotel personnel were quizzed extensively by Julian Crosby, who knew his reputation was on the line. He knew he'd need to justify himself to the police, and it was vital for him to alleviate any trace of his own involvement with Mr Vickers. All his staff feared for their livelihoods. He was ferocious in his questioning, convinced there had to be at least one bad apple in the box, turning a blind eye to comings and goings in the foyer of his luxury establishment.

He concentrated on the night staff, and eventually two hapless night porters caved in under the pressure, and were dismissed on the spot, Julian Crosby passing their names onto the police officers who were hounding him. They were still trying to link a connection between Mr Crosby and the dead man, feeling it was an important coincidence which could not be overlooked

Along with the workforce at The Beirut Grange, these two young porters were questioned at length, each claiming to have been lured by the colossal amount of money offered to look the other way, when non-residents walked over to the lift servicing the penthouse suite.

Jaaved Boutros broke down in his interview in a torrent of grief, admitting to his relationship with Richard Vickers, who, he stated, had promised to leave his wife so they could be together, but also conceded he was unsure if Helen knew of his intentions.

Inspector Kitely, had not as yet, had the chance to question Helen Vickers again, but was sure that would be rectified just as soon as New Scotland Yard were on the case.

At Starlington Hall, Lady Lizbum was sitting on one of the comfy sofas in the back snug, half-heartedly drinking a cup of Earl Grey tea, and mulling things over. Lord Duncan and Toby had taken two of the horses for a hack along the bridle paths at the back of the estate. She had settled down to watch an afternoon quiz show, but her thoughts kept drifting, troubling memories from the past resurfacing. She remembered back to when the affair with Richard had restarted not long into her marriage. It was brief, and ended when her feelings of guilt towards her husband and Helen, started to overwhelm her. He'd made overtures over the years to rekindle their liaison, and she'd had to show a great deal of restraint to stop from falling for his charismatic charm all over again. He was a hard man to refuse, and a powerful one to boot. She had a particularly vivid recollection of a summer's day not too many years ago when a weekend house party was in full swing. Due to a shared interest in horticulture, she and Richard had been walking around the experimental wild garden together. It lay just behind the beech hedge, at the back of the house to the right, in an area which eventually led on to the wooded part of the estate. She and Colin Armstrong had been working side by side on the joint project and she was somewhat proud of the results.

'Come on, Pip,' Richard said seductively. 'How about a grope for old times' sake?' And he'd pulled her into a clinch without warning, unfocused by whisky and boldness.

'Behave Richard,' she said, grappling light-heartedly. 'Let's quash that idea. You've had far too much to drink, and we'd both regret it by the end of the day,' she said, laughingly.

She heard a nervous cough, and then looked up to see Jessica, Antony's fiancée, standing on the other side of the hedge where an archway had been formed to give access to the wild garden.

They pulled apart quickly, but not before Jessica, unable to hide her embarrassment, had said in a high, strangled voice, 'Oh, hello, I didn't know you had the same idea as me. The wild flowers are looking splendid, Philippa, such an array of colour. I'd just come out to admire your handiwork.'

Richard gave a hearty guffaw, thinking it highly amusing. Philippa's colour was rising, and Jessica, whose skin had the dark enchanting hue of an august peach, looked like a rabbit in headlights.

'Yes, it's coming along,' said Philippa, haltingly. 'I love the poppies best, how about you, Jessica, which are your favourites?'

'Erm, I think it's the cornflowers, but they're all so pretty it's hard to choose.'

'Well, I'm going in, I'll leave you to discuss the merits of wild flowers, if you'll excuse me, ladies,' said Richard, mockingly. He turned on his heels, retreating to the safety of the lawns leading round to the front terrace to join the rest of the party.

'Would you like to wander through on your own, Jess? Do pick some blooms to take home with you, my dear. Help yourself. I think I'll join the others now.'

Philippa, having regained her composure, walked slowly back towards the house.

She was in a welter of nerves for weeks, distressed in case Jessica should tell Antony or Helen about her discovery.

But as time went on she realised that no feeling of discomfort was ever felt around Antony, his mother or indeed Jessica. That's one of the reasons why Philippa had been so very fond of her. She'd been dreadfully upset when Jessica had met with her untimely end. Jessica had kept her counsel, and Philippa felt nothing but respect and gratitude towards the young lady for being discreet.

So, now with investigations under way, a whip of self-loathing struck at her, as she feared the truth would surely surface and show its ugly face again.

Helen had been informed that the body could finally be released from the morgue, and she could go ahead with arranging the delayed funeral.

With all the new information coming forward, Helen was once again forced into the interview room, now at New Scotland Yard. The officers assigned to the case had done their best to unveil the facts to the widow in a sensitive way, but there was no denying that the unpalatable disclosures had been met with shock and revulsion. Helen admitted to knowing her husband had been unfaithful, and that she'd been suspicious he'd met someone special recently, but was clearly dumbfounded to find his lover was the same sex as himself.

This information was the final straw for Helen. She now felt a seething anger towards Richard. She felt humiliated, foolish and used. How on earth would she be able to face his funeral? She'd been assured that none of the sordid details would reach the press, who had all stopped reporting further on the case for the time being, but she knew in the fullness of time the distasteful truth may eventually come out.

She felt the need to talk things over with someone outside of her immediate family, and instantly thought of Philippa and Duncan. 'Hang the bloody funeral arrangements,' she thought, as she tapped in the familiar telephone number with a vengeance.

'Good morning, Starlington Hall,' said the confident voice of Lord Duncan.

'Duncan,' started Helen. 'May I come to see you today? I need to speak with you both.'

'Of course you can, my dear. Is all well?' he replied, picking up on the stern tone.

'No, it is not. I won't speak now. I'll pack a few things and be with you later. I shall travel by train. I'll let you know my arrival time when I know it myself.'

'Okey dokey, Helen. We'll look forward to seeing you later.'

Duncan quickly tracked down his wife to tell her the news, and they drove together, later in the day, to collect Helen from the train station, both feeling decidedly jumpy.

Helen chose to wait until they were back in Starlington Hall before divulging the news, so they all made small talk, until settled in front of the log fire, with a pot of coffee at the ready.

She came straight out with it. 'Did either of you know that Richard was gay?'

'Good heavens no!' exclaimed Philippa.

'Gay?' spoke Duncan. 'Not on your life, Helen. I always thought of him as a "ladies' man" We've learnt a few things from Colin Armstrong, our gardener, which we were waiting for the right time to tell you, Helen, but, well, regarding your question, no, I had no idea, my dear.'

'Duncan, do stop bleating,' put in Philippa.

'I realise I didn't know the man I was married to at all. It was all a facade and I find, instead of feeling upset and distraught, all I feel is rage. And I've been told I can go ahead and arrange his funeral. Well I can tell you now, the way I feel I wouldn't care if he was buried in a ditch. The humiliation is too much,' she finished, tears of anger threatening. Determined not to give in to them she carried on. 'How can I be expected to reconcile myself to it all?'

The two stunned friends were initially struck dumb.

'Now, come on, Helen, you're a strong woman. We'll give you a hand with organising everything. You could have a very quiet family burial or cremation. Just you and close family,' suggested Philippa.

'I know you won't want to accept this at the moment, Helen,' started Duncan, timidly. He'd toyed with keeping his mouth shut, but felt he owed it to his old buddy to speak up on his behalf. 'In Richard's defence, I would like to say this. His job was exceptionally demanding. There were decisions he and I had to make, which would keep any man from sleeping soundly. There needed to be some sort of release. We all had to find a way of coping. Though it sounds sordid and shameful to you right now, maybe, in time, you may understand, Helen, and learn to forgive,' finished Duncan, who had spoken out of character and candidly, from the heart.

'My, Duncan, that was quite a speech,' said Lady Lizbum. 'We women are not as stupid as we may look, actually, and I expect Helen would agree. I don't doubt that you both had your diversions, and methods of "release". But for the moment I, for one, certainly sympathise with Helen's sentiments. None of us wish to feel humiliated, and I understand entirely how she must be feeling right now.'

'That's exactly it, Pip, I just feel so stupid. In time I may learn to forgive, Duncan, but not yet.'

In another part of the house, Toby Soames was staring out of the window in a kind of stupor. He'd become restless and bored, being cooped up with his parents for weeks on end, wanting to get back to Africa, his family and job. He wasn't good at relaxing, and needed his brain to be stimulated, or challenged, instead of languishing around with no purpose. There were only so many times he could go out for a good gallop or take the dogs for a walk to the pub. He felt frustrated, constantly waiting and hoping to hear news through his father. There didn't seem to be much progress being made on the Richard Vickers case. If only he'd been able to speak to Richard about Kellan and the twins, things could have been so different. He made up his mind to go and stay with his brother. He knew Will had very little space on his boat, but they could rough it together, as they'd done when they were boys. Yes, that's what he'd do, hop on a train to the capital. It was a long time since he'd been in London. He loved the buzz of a big city, so he looked down at his phone, found the contact number he needed and made the call.

Meanwhile, back in Dorset on the following day, Paula and Nicky, having almost completed the collection, decided on a little treat. They would shut up the barn for a couple of hours and take themselves off to a nice little pub for an extended lunch hour.

They chose to go to one of their favourite places, in the heart of the countryside, where the food and ambience were equally good. There was always a cluster of donkeys outside, their winter coats tangled with mud, and their faces forlorn. As the two women walked up the pathway, the stubborn creatures made no effort to move, so they diverted around a couple of wooden tables and benches in order to enter the establishment.

Once inside, they found a table by the window. It wasn't long before they were tucking into their meals.

Out of the window, they spotted a familiar face, pushing his way past the donkeys and into the pub, a newspaper tucked under his arm.

He looked around for a vacant table, and caught sight of Paula and Nicky, waving at him.

'What a lovely surprise, ladies,' he said, making his way to their table. 'Would you mind if I joined you?'

'Of course not, Anton,' said Nicky.

When Antony had secured a pint and a meal order, he joined his friends, abandoning his newspaper to the spare chair, to read another time.

'Hey, how are you both?'

'Well, thanks, Antony,' said Paula. 'How are things with you?'

'Oh, you know, I'm OK. Mother has had the go ahead for the funeral, so I'll be very relieved to get that over with now.'

'Do you have a date yet, Antony?'

Yes. It is to be November 26th. After much debate, we've decided on a simple funeral for immediate family only in Richmond. Then on the 28th there will be a thanksgiving service at the village church in Starlington, followed by a reception back at the hall. Mother couldn't face having to arrange it all. After much persuasion, she's agreed to go ahead with this arrangement. I hope you may be able to attend?'

'We'll need to check the diary, but we can usually switch things around if necessary.'

Hesitating slightly Nicky added, 'Do you know if Lisa will be joining you?'

'Yes, actually, she has agreed to accompany me. We've … spoken about… our situation at long last, and have agreed it's not working for either of us, which is a relief I must confess, but she seems keen to attend the service to lend support.'

'That's good to hear, Antony. I'm pleased you'll have someone to lean on,' said Nicky, a little awkwardly.

'Then I can start to get on with my life again. It's been a rough ride, and it's not over yet, but I'm determined to make a fresh start after the funeral. Talking of which,' said Anton, turning towards the woman on his left with a grin, 'how about that curry I promised you. When can we fit that in, Nicky?'

CHAPTER TWENTY

On speaking to their client, Paula and Nicky had agreed on a mutually convenient date in their respective calendars for the very final fittings. They planned to go to the estate on the 26th November, spend the following day on the collection, and then subsequently stay for the service, therefore, for the intervening time Nicky and Paula knew they must work towards this deadline.

There were one or two garments which were proving tricky. Paula had sourced some vintage fabrics, one being a fabulously colourful paisley pattern. However, Nicky was finding the design difficult to match up and she could be heard from her sewing bench cussing from time to time. Paula kept her head down during these tense times, and the other vintage fabric, with a cute but tricky seaside themed pattern, was also trying Nicky's patience. They'd had to order over the Internet, so it was a bit hit and miss as to whether the fabric would be to their liking, and quality. With many companies now bringing out fabrics imitating original "vintage" prints, they'd taken quite a risky punt.

'Blimey,' said Nicky. 'I hadn't realised the amount of pattern matching needed. It's a good job we over ordered. It's like a whole new art. I hope it works. I think it will, Paula, in fact I have a feeling we could be on to a whole new line.'

'Hallelujah, thank the Lord. I was beginning to regret

suggesting it,' said Paula, relieved to hear her chum's endorsement.

'No, it was a great idea, it just needs patience. I'm getting the hang of it now, look,' she said, holding up her latest creation.

'It's a work of art, Nicky, you're a genius. I just love that unusual bias binding and your signature stitching. Come on, let's have a break, it's lunch time. I'm sick of this computer.'

They both went into the kitchen to start chopping up the ingredients for the salad, slicing the bread, making a simple dressing, then setting it out to their satisfaction.

Sitting down at the small kitchen table to eat their lunch, the kettle on for a cup of tea to follow, their thoughts turned to recent events.

'So, how did Leonard react when you told him Poppy is coming home for Christmas?'

'Over the moon, as you'd expect. He's really looking forward to seeing her.'

'And, dare I ask? Have you decided to tell her about her father?'

'Yes, I have,' said Nicky, decisively. 'Maybe it's after all the facts that have come out about Richard recently. I now realise that how I went about choosing to have a one-night stand with a gorgeous Italian count, purposely hoping I'd become pregnant, isn't exactly the crime of the century.'

'Of course it's not, Nicky. The fact you wanted a child but not a man was no one's business but yours. It was your own decision to go it alone, and now that she's older I'm sure she'll understand, and respect you for it too.'

'We'll have to wait and see on that one. She may, of course, wish to track Christo down. That could definitely open up a hornets' nest for sure, but I'll have to face that in due course. I'm pleased to have come to the decision at any rate. The rest is in the lap of the Gods so to speak.'

'That's a good plan, and well done you, for being brave.'

'What are you up to tonight, Paula?'

'Oh, nothing much, I'll just be pondering on what to take on our next road trip!'

'I know, we'll both have to be thinking about what to wear to the church, and then there are all the rest of the bits and pieces we seem to be lumbered with every time we set off. It feels like we're no sooner home than we're off up to Hampshire again. Never mind, we're nearly on the home run.'

Driving home from the barn, Paula thought in advance to the difficult evening ahead. She knew time had run out for her and her young lover. He'd been invited back to the marital home by his estranged wife, and Paula was definitely not standing in his way. She'd known this day would come from the very start. Even though she'd encouraged it, and thought she'd be brave, now the time was drawing close to them saying goodbye, she felt saddened, though determined not to let him see. She knew she would let him go with love in her heart.

What she hadn't prepared for was what happened next. She'd always believed they would remain friends, so when she arrived home after noticing a missed call from him, she checked her voicemail. His voice sounded strange, distant and cold. He said he couldn't see her tonight, on what would have been their last night together, because he knew he would be unable to resist her. He explained, awkwardly, with a voice she didn't recognise, that he felt it was better to cut all ties, and asked her not to contact him again. She felt devastated at the sudden change in his demeanour, and when she tried to call him, his number was unobtainable.

So that was it, she thought, anguished at the childish way he'd behaved. No real goodbye, just a voicemail, after all they'd meant to each other. She refused to believe he'd not felt the same, and knew in her heart his emotions had been just as strong as hers. She had to concede it was probably because of the difference in their ages. He wasn't mature enough to face the final goodbye. She found a release in the tears which had been threatening, and gave in to them willingly, and once underway, all her mercurial thoughts came flooding back. The pet names they'd used (Lady Chatterley and Mellors), corny she knew, but decidedly fitting. The expression of their spiritual beliefs, the long debates, the laughter, the books and places they'd travelled to separately in the past, which they discussed at length. But above all, it was the love. A multitude of unique memories held between the two. Paula knew over the coming weeks that she would hold the ache of loneliness close, and the pain of parting, which could only be borne in isolation. She had no one to blame but herself. She knew she'd get over him in time, but for now it hurt like hell. She felt exhausted and spent as the torrent of grief eventually subsided, and Paula climbed slowly up to her bedroom and into her desolate bed. With swollen eyes and a feeling of hopelessness she fell into a fatigued slumber.

There followed a fitful night's sleep from which she woke with a pitifully heavy heart.

She arrived at the barn on the morning of the 26th well

ahead of Nicky. When Nicky pulled into the gravel forecourt, most of the collection was already packed neatly into the boot of Paula's car.

She tried hard to act as naturally as she could, but felt as flat as a pancake. She was a strong woman who would get over her broken heart in her own inimitable way. 'OK,' she thought, 'let's just concentrate on the next few days,' as she pulled out onto the road.

'You're a bit quiet, Paula, is everything all right?' asked a perceptive Nicky as she sat in the passenger seat next to her good friend.

'Me, oh yes, I'm just concentrating on getting you there in one piece, Nicky.'

'Well, as long as you're all right,' said Nicky, doubtfully.

'So, I wonder what New Scotland Yard will have discovered about Richard Vickers?'

Paula knew she had to force herself into the present moment instead of ruminating on her loss, so jolted herself out of her reverie, making a sterling effort to concentrate.

'Right, yes, I wonder. We don't know if they've found out how the crime was even committed do we?'

'No. But I suppose they must know that by now surely. How would *we* get to know, though? I wonder if they ever tell the family of any progress or just keep it to themselves. Antony hasn't mentioned anything to me recently anyway.'

'Well we'll just have to keep going I suppose.'

Feeling a touch of humour was needed, Nicky took on a strange accent, a cross between someone from *Allo, Allo* and an English professor. 'I weel 'av to employ the leetle grey cells, Captain 'Astings!'

Paula burst into laughter, despite herself and they carried

on in this vein for the next few miles.

After a while the long driveway of Starlington Hall came into sight. The newly sparse heavy clutch of trees loomed before them; the autumnal leaves all but vanished from view. Winter was upon them, warm coats, gloves and scarves the new order of the day.

On entering the familiar vestibule and being greeted by Vivienne, the two dogs bounded up to the girls, and they felt thrilled to find themselves being recognised by the two mutts, who were wagging their tails enthusiastically.

'Hello Horatio and Marmaduke,' said Paula, bending down to pet them both zealously. 'Oh, Marmaduke, have you hurt your paw?' she said, noticing a nasty gash.

'Yes, he's been digging where he shouldn't have been, in the flower bed at the front of the terrace. He got a good telling off by His Lordship, didn't you, boy?' said Vivienne, joining in with the petting.

'There must have been something sharp for him to get such a deep cut,' remarked Nicky.

'Yes, I suppose so,' said Vivienne. 'Lord Duncan took him to the vet and he had a few stitches, I believe. He's limping rather badly, but I reckon he's enjoyed the bit of extra fussing.'

'Well we all like a bit of fussing from time to time, eh, boy? Anyway, we'd better head upstairs with our bags. Are we in the same room as before, Vivienne?'

'Yes, it seems to have a new name, that room. It's now referred to as the Gingham and Velvet room!'

'Ha, fancy us having a room named after us... we're honoured.'

'Lunch will be served at one o clock, ladies. Lord and

Lady Soames are in Romsey. They send their apologies, but will be back in time for lunch. I've made a nice shepherd's pie.'

'That sounds wonderful, Vivienne. Thanks.'

After settling in again, unpacking and depositing the finished collection in the dressing room, Nicky and Paula decided once again to take a turn around the grounds.

On seeing the soil still spilling out of the new bed which they assumed Barker had not got round to finishing, suddenly Paula noticed something gleaming, shining out, and being of a curious nature, she walked over to it, going down on her haunches to have a closer look.

'Nicky, come here,' she said excitedly. 'We need a spade. Let's see if there's one in the greenhouse.'

'What is it, what have you found, Paula?'

'Let's get the spade first,' she said, walking quickly over to the greenhouse.

They located a small trowel and spade then headed back to the area near the terrace.

Paula, having shown her friend the large shard of glass she'd found, bent down and started to carefully remove the soil, with Nicky now doing the same. After digging for a while, much deeper down, they both looked at each other, eyes wide and disbelieving.

They carefully made a pile of their haul: a pile of broken glass, which couldn't be identified as anything in particular, one port glass with a stout stem, still intact, and a small neat but very badly chipped decanter. Both of these had now filled up with soil and debris, but were unmistakably not historical relics from ancient times. Then Nicky spotted a bright piece of something which shone a different hue from the rest. It was a dull red. It may have been a garnet or ruby, or it could just as easily have been a piece of coloured glass.

'What is that, do you think?' she asked, holding it in the palm of her hand.

'I'm not sure if that's of any significance Nicky, but all this other stuff looks very suspicious indeed. How did the police miss it?'

'I reckon that's what poor old Marmaduke cut his paw on. He's gone and disturbed the soil enough for you to spot the shard of glass. I can't believe The Twizzler didn't spot it.'

'We need to get it all on a sheet of some kind and inform the police.'

Nicky still had the coloured glass in her hand. 'What about this?'

'I don't think it will do any harm for you to hang onto that, but let's get this lot sorted out first.'

Nicky pocketed the red stone, and followed Paula in through the side door which led to the back hallway, up the stairs and into the dressing room where they found a spare length of material and a large bag.

Carefully handling the items and placing them on the material, then into the bag, they took it into the back snug to discuss their next move.

'So, the poison must have been poured into the port glass from the small decanter. I wonder if traces of poison can still be found on them. Wow, Nicky, this is an amazing find. Do you think fingerprints would still be on there? If so, then we're in the frame!'

'How spooky to think we may have just discovered the vital evidence needed to solve the case. Maybe we should wait before informing the police until we've spoken to Lady Lizbum and The Twizzler?'

'Yes, we should definitely wait. Mind you, well, I hate to say it, but what if one of them is the murderer? I mean, we can't rule anyone out at this point can we?'

'I know what you're saying, but, well I guess they'd have to brazen it out wouldn't they? I don't see any way round it, Paula. It would be rude for us to go behind their backs when we're staying here…'

The conversation at lunch time, therefore, whilst munching their way through an excellent shepherd's pie, peas and pointed cabbage, followed by a winter trifle, was entirely focussed on the girls' "find".

The Twizzler took charge and did all the telephoning. The local police were called in once again, initiated by orders from New Scotland Yard, who instructed them to investigate promptly at Starlington Hall.

Lady Lizbum, Nicky and Paula spent the following day in the dressing room, Her Ladyship trying on garment after garment, each one meeting with ooohs and aaahs, as they made their way through the successful "collection". Having been so meticulous in their measuring and preparation, everything fit her like a glove, and when the final garment in the range was stepped into, the girls sat back in wonder.

It was the evening gown for the gala dinner, and she looked remarkable.

The fabric, after much deliberation, was soft silk brocade in the palest gold, embroidered with tiny gold roses, and a café au lait underskirt. The fitted bodice had very fine pleating in the middle, continuing all the way through to the full-length skirt, and ending with a fish tail hem. The whole ensemble accentuated Lady Lizbum's long sleek body.

Both women felt unexpectedly overwhelmed as Philippa paraded through the dressing room as if on a catwalk, each feeling a strange mix of pride and relief.

'You have excelled yourselves, ladies. How can I ever thank you enough?' said the lady of the house, her own eyes now unexpectedly starting to fill.

'It's thanks enough for us that you are happy, Philippa,' said Paula quietly.

'Well, even though we have an onerous task ahead of us all tomorrow, tonight we can celebrate my collection along with my boys, who will be joining us. They've been together in London, having a rare old time. So, yes, tonight we'll have a small celebratory dinner and try to put tomorrow's events to the back of our minds.'

CHAPTER TWENTY-ONE

Whilst preparing for the night ahead Paula received a call from Freddy.

'Hello Sherlock, Watson here,' he started. 'I have news for you. I've been checking up on those infamous parties. It seems they've been going on for years, in one venue or another. Richard Vickers was quite a player, Paula, he must have been making a wad of cash too. One name keeps coming up; Julian Crosby. Seemingly he's the one who provides the venue. He has a string of hotels both in the capital and all over the south of England, and guess what? He was at Starlington Hall on the night of the murder, as you must surely know?'

'Crikey, Freddy, yes, he was. I recall him being a bit of a pain to be honest, sucking up to everyone in quite a galling way. I could tell the other men weren't keen on him, but I don't remember him speaking to Richard particularly, in fact, there was no indication they were acquainted. Hmm, that's a bit suspicious in itself. I think he's new to the village and he struck me as wanting to get in with the "county set". Well, well, how interesting. There must be a connection, however vague. That's just too much of a coincidence. It's food for thought, Freddy, definitely food for thought. Thanks for your input.'

'Are you free this evening? I thought we may grab a bite

to eat?'

'No, Freddy, I'm sorry. I'm up at the hall, just about to go down to dinner.'

'How the other half lives, eh?'

'Well I'm not looking forward to tomorrow; it's the service in the village church for Richard Vickers. I think it may be a difficult day.'

'Well, I hope the information may prove useful. I'll catch up soon.'

'Yes, thanks again. I'll give you a call next week.'

'OK, bye for now, Paula.'

Paula hit the red button and turned to Nicky to fill her in.

'How interesting, I wonder if there were money issues between Julian and Richard. Or blackmail? They certainly hid their relationship, or partnership well; I wouldn't have guessed they were familiar with each other.'

'Nor me, Nicky. The plot thickens eh? He may have been in on the party scene, but if not, he must have had an idea what was going on. Julian Crosby could have easily been blackmailing Richard, him being quite high profile 'n all. Anyhow, we'd better head downstairs now. Are you finished? You look lovely, by the way.'

'Thanks. I wasn't expecting a big swanky dinner tonight, but I think I'll "do".'

Knocking on the dining room door, and entering, Nicky and Paula were greeted like long lost friends by Toby and Will.

'How was London?' asked Nicky of Toby.

'Really great, thanks. The accommodation was decidedly "bijou" but charming, and the neighbours were a hoot,' replied Toby, laughing. 'I loved it. It was just what the doctor ordered.'

Lady Lizbum held her tongue, not wishing to start the evening on a sour note. She still had difficulty reconciling herself to William's lifestyle.

'So,' said William who was sat next to Paula. 'I hear you've made a discovery. What a turn-up for the books. It shouldn't be long now before the game's up. You two gals are certainly full of surprises,' noted Will.

'Do you know, Duncan, if they've been able to identify the fingerprints yet?' asked Nicky.

'No, my dear, I am not party to their investigations.'

'Well I suppose it all depends on that. Maybe the fingerprints were wiped off at the time, we'll just have to wait and see won't we?' said Paula.

'I've always been fascinated with forensics,' put in Nicky. 'My daughter, Poppy, was keen at one point to pursue it as a career. She may still decide she wants to train. Did I tell you she will be back home in time for Christmas?'

'That's wonderful news, Nicky. You must be thrilled,' said Philippa.

'I most certainly am.'

'And will your daughter be joining you at Christmas, Paula?'

'Yes, she will. Tegan has a chaotic agenda but she always makes sure she's with us at Christmas.'

William looked towards Paula again, feeling a little tug to his heartstrings. 'It would be so great to have a son or daughter to spend the festive season with,' he thought. It was one of the few times of the year when he regretted not being a family man.

Toby was also pondering on where he would be for the

festive season.

There was a loaded silence around the table now, all six people mulling over their own views on the subject.

'Right, well,' started Duncan. 'We have to get through tomorrow first. I hope then we can start to put all this wretched business behind us.'

'Well, yes, I for one would like to make a toast to 'Gingham and Velvet, and Ma's superb collection,' said Will, raising his glass.

They all did the same thing, and the glasses chinked together charmingly.

'How do you know it's superb when you haven't even seen it Will?' laughed Nicky.

'I just 'ave a feeling in me bones, me dear,' replied Will, touching his nose, and adopting the tone of a dithery old man.

The morning of the service of thanksgiving for the life of Richard Vickers was grey and overcast. All the residents of Starlington Hall were up early so as to be at the village church in good time.

Nicky and Paula had been awake for some time, drinking tea and ruminating on their findings of the previous day.

Suddenly there came a high-pitched scream from the dressing room. Nicky and Paula rushed along the corridor to see Philippa standing in her dressing gown with the summer coat, still on its hanger, held at arm's length. She had a look of horror on her face.

'Look, all the fastenings have been cut off,' she said, turning to the girls. 'Do you know anything about this, ladies?'

'No. It was still intact when we gave it back to you.

Where did you find it?'

'I was going through my wardrobe in search of my charcoal suit and I found the coat in the middle of my grey section. As you know I have my clothes colour coordinated which is why I noticed it, amongst my dark clothes. It stood out as you can imagine. Did you show it to anyone else?' she said accusingly.

'No, we didn't, I can promise you. We brought it back on the weekend of the shoot, and put it in its place in your wardrobe, in the correct section of colours,' said Paula. 'What were the fastenings, Philippa? Where did they come from? Do they have a name? And have you looked for them anywhere else in here?'

'I believe they're called netsuke. My aunt spent time in Japan, and brought them back from one of her trips. Why would anyone be interested in them, I wonder? And who could have been so cruel as to cut them off, ruining my favourite coat. I'm at a complete loss, it's beyond the pale. No, there's no sign of them anywhere else, as far as I can tell, though I haven't had time yet to do a thorough search.'

'Well, it would have to be someone with access to your wardrobes, but I can assure you, Philippa, it wasn't us,' put in Nicky.

'Well, I don't lock this door as you know, and I can't believe Mrs Armstrong would do such a thing,' said Philippa. 'This needs further investigation, but for now we'll have to leave it, and get on. We're running out of time. I still need to get dressed. I'm sorry if I was sharp, but it was a terrible shock.'

'It's OK, we understand. Yes, come on, let's leave this until later,' said Paula. 'Do you have your suit?'

'Yes, here it is. I'll just choose a blouse and put this coat back for the time being,' she replied, distractedly.

Nicky and Paula, flustered and shaken by the episode in the dressing room, returned to their room and started their preparations for the day ahead. When they'd finished showering, dressing and putting on their make-up, Paula got out her "tablet" and proceeded to locate something on Google.

'Whatever are you doing, Paula? We don't have time for the Internet,' said Nicky, brusquely.

'Just a quick five minutes, ah yes, here we are… Nicky, come here, I can't believe it, look at this… it's unbelievable.'

The girls had another reason for gasping, open-mouthed at what came into view on the small screen.

'What does it mean?'

The village church was packed to the rafters with family, friends, associates of Richard Vickers, and villagers. There was a strong police presence standing at the back of the church. The music chosen was dramatic and haunting, and the vicar did a sterling job in his sermon, surprisingly managing to evoke a mood of serenity, which couldn't have been easy in the circumstances.

Paula and Nicky noticed Jaaved Boutros sitting discreetly in a pew at the very back of the church, looking nervous and sad, but also fearful. They saw him slip out discreetly at the end of the service, and felt relieved to see him disappear, having been anxious in case he may have thought to make a scene.

Helen broke with tradition and did not stand shaking hands with anyone after the service. She simply made her way to the funeral car, supported by Antony and Isobel, and gave instructions to the driver, to depart to Starlington Hall.

Lord Duncan had suggested they hire outside caterers for the reception, but on mentioning his plan to Vivienne Armstrong had been met with such fierce opposition, he felt like he'd recommended they offer the job to serial killers. Vivienne saw it as the ultimate insult, and so he conceded, allowing her and her small team to busy themselves in the well-equipped kitchen of Starlington Hall in order to prepare an excellent buffet.

When Paula and Nicky arrived, the house was filling up with the catering team, all smartly dressed, on hand to offer schooners of sherry and soft drinks.

The guests were spreading themselves between the vestibule and drawing room. Whilst mingling with the people they'd met over the weekend of the shoot, both women felt the need to be observant, and polite, as opposed to jovial and friendly. They also had the feeling everyone else was acting in the same way. It made for some rather stilted conversations, and feelings of unease amongst the visitors. Everyone seemed to be on their best behaviour.

The local police had been joined by a clutch of officers from New Scotland Yard, and although none were uniformed, somehow, by their very demeanour, they seemed to stick out like high court judges in a juggling contest,. They were on top alert, aware this was a good opportunity to observe the guests in repose, so to speak.

Julian Crosby's voice could be heard rising above the rest of the room, in an obvious effort to strike an impact. He gave the impression that he never gave up on the idea of fawning over the nobility. His youngish wife, looked pale and strained, and followed in his wake, like a feeble shadow, noticeably embarrassed by her husband's conduct.

Helen was finding it gruelling to intermingle, and rigidly placed herself by the flanks of her son and daughter. It was evident she couldn't cope with having to converse with anyone else.

Nicky and Paula found themselves in a group of familiar faces, when all of a sudden, Nicky spotted something which made her eyes blink rapidly beneath her curved brows, and her heart quicken. Like a beacon shining from a lighthouse, what she observed stood out, and almost rooted her to the spot. She turned her startled eyes towards Paula, who was initially oblivious to her friend's dilemma. When Paula finally cottoned onto the gaze Nicky was giving her, she discreetly drew her aside.

'What is it?'

'I've seen something. Don't draw attention, you must remain cool, Paula. We need to join the group again, and then you need to follow my eyes. Whatever you do, don't react. Keep calm and be discreet. We'll casually make our exit when the time is right to report to the police. Don't rush me, just keep talking about anything you can think of, and whatever you do don't make it obvious. A lot depends on this.'

They joined in with the banter of the group again. Thankfully no one had overheard the exchange, or realised the impact of Nicky's words. At an opportune moment, Paula watched Nicky's cautious stare, and noticed the object which had caused Nicky's heart to skip a beat. It was all Paula could do to steady herself. But, with nerves of steel, she held it together, though her legs felt like jelly.

When it looked as if the group were starting to disperse naturally, they both moved as slowly and artlessly as they could to the far side of the room. They managed to exit discreetly, disappearing behind the door, and then high tailing it to the nearest policeman, who directed them to the top detective, in the library.

A little while later, having had a long discussion with the girls from Gingham and Velvet, and now in receipt of certain facts, the chief police officer gave them the go ahead.

The girls rushed upstairs to the floral room to retrieve the items they needed. They hastily collected them together, and walked coolly down the stairs, being careful not to draw any attention. Stepping into the library, they handed over the vital pieces of the jigsaw to the police team. The chief inspector from New Scotland Yard, was very impressed with the vigilant pair.

The police personnel then set to work on the large table, carefully piecing together all the valuable evidence which had been provided, knowing they would need to be meticulous in getting this next part of the operation wholly correct and watertight.

Along with the forensic results of the fingerprints, it had all begun to fall into place.

The girls returned to the drawing room and helped themselves to another schooner of sherry each, gulping it down greedily, and chatting inanely to each other about anything that came to mind.

Before any of the guests started to take their leave, the police officer in charge of the case drew Lord Soames aside, and ordered His Lordship to accompany him to the library, where he outlined what he intended to do.

His instructions were clear and concise. He needed to see all the people who had been there at the murder scene, on the weekend of the shooting party, to congregate in the drawing room. It was no mean feat, but with the help of his discreet and loyal staff, Lord Soames managed to complete the mission.

With all the other funeral guests having now left, the remaining ones who had been in attendance on the night of the banquet were now seated in the drawing room. This included the hired help of Colin and Vivienne Armstrong, along with Verity and Rosalind Barnes.

The door opened and in walked the senior officer from New Scotland Yard.

'Ladies and gentlemen, I'm sure you must realise why I have gathered you all together. The murder of Richard Vickers has proved a complicated case, with many twists and turns. Richard Vickers was indeed a complex man, with a lot of secrets which we have needed to unearth,' he stated dramatically.

'It has taken a long time to untangle the web of lies and deceit which have led to this meeting.'

He looked around at the circle of suspects, scanning the stunned faces, knowing they all had something to hide. There was an air of anticipation, and the term "you could hear a pin drop" was a very apt one.

'We are now very close to being in a position to make an arrest.'

The faces seated around the drawing room of Starlington Hall all wore a grave and solemn expression. Some folk automatically sat forwards, whilst others sank back further into their places.

After scanning the sea of faces the senior officer, who had been made aware of whom he was searching for, came to rest on a certain person.

'Firstly, I would like to take a look at the very distinguishable accessory you are wearing please,' he announced, bending forwards to indicate the piece.

Everyone in the room stared at the back of the person, who had reluctantly stood up and was now following the officer to his table. The item was removed and handed over. There was a bewildered look on the faces of the rest of the circle, who were all wondering what the gold and ruby adornment had to do with the outcome.

The individual walked back to the original chair with as much dignity as could be mustered.

The officer brought out a small gemstone from a small bowl sitting on the table. He easily pressed it into the gaping hole which lay in the midst of the cluster of rubies, and laid it back on the table.

'Ah, yes, a perfect match.'

Gradually a hush descended on the drawing room, as all eyes came to rest on the anxious being.

That's when they knew they were beaten.

CHAPTER TWENTY-TWO

Less than two years previously, there was a chance meeting which was to spiral into a chain of events leading to this moment.

Two strangers had decided to attend an evening class on business studies, at the local college. It turned out to be a short-lived foray into the world of study for one of them. Having been raised on a rough council estate, on the edge of the town, the eldest of six children, with an alcoholic mother and a father who drifted in and out of their life and jail with equal measure, life was pretty dismal.

On that first evening, one of the two walked tentatively into the cold, bleak classroom, feeling like an outsider and a fraud. A welcoming young lady, who had arrived earlier, looked up from her place in the classroom, and smiled. Unused to social niceties, the first person, taken unawares, had managed to return a thin smile, however, it hadn't reached her eyes.

Against all the odds, though, these two women became close friends. Jessica and Lisa.

It didn't take Lisa long to drop out of the course, unable to maintain her attention span, but she became fascinated by Jessica and her set of friends.

She learned that Jessica lived in London from Tuesday to

Friday, and was being sponsored for the night school by her employers, the prestigious Christie's auction house. Lisa, who regularly spent time in the capital herself, but was careful not to disclose any hint of this, was surprised that Jessica would attend a course in this provincial college, given her present circumstances.

It transpired Jessica had managed to persuade her boss to let her study the business course at her local college, to allow more time with her fiancé at the weekends. She used Monday during the day for further research. Her speciality was Japanese artefacts, and she was a rising star at Christie's, but needed a business qualification to progress further.

Lisa was careful to keep her background hidden from Jessica and Antony. There was always an excuse forthcoming, when any mention was made of them being introduced to her family. She spun tales of a widowed mother, who was too delicate to receive visitors. She was very adept at avoidance tactics, and lying had become her natural default setting.

'Going to meet your posh friends, eh, our Lisa?' teased Shane, one of her unsavoury brothers.

'It's none of your business. What's it to you, anyway?'

'When are you going to bring them home to meet the family?' he smirked.

'Just you stay out of my life and get on with your own miserable existence.'

'What do you think they'd say if they knew the real Lisa Moore, eh?' he said, with a threatening undertone.

'I'm warning you, Shane. Back off.'

'I wonder what little Miss Prim would think about what you get up to in the city, huh, you answer me that?'

Lisa faced her brother, eye to eye, trembling now with fury. 'You just watch your mouth, you lowdown scum.'

'Oh yes, miss hoity toity, it's all right for you now, lording it above the rest of us, but you mark my words, I'll be the one you come running to when you need my help, and mark my words, one day you will.'

Looking back, now, in the drawing room of Starlington Hall, Lisa closed her eyes tight, remembering his words.

One day, after the friends had been seeing each other regularly, Lisa popped in to see Jessica unexpectedly. She was sitting in her lounge, lost in her work on the computer, concentrating on the job in hand.

'Don't stop your work, Jess. I was just passing and wondered if you were free. Carry on. What are you looking at?' Lisa asked, more out of obligation, than genuine curiosity.

'Actually, this is very interesting, Lisa. Pull up a chair and have a gander.' On the screen were a series of images, small intricate carvings, made out of what looked like ivory, depicting tiny Japanese people, Japanese characters (writings), and oriental scenes, They were beautiful, and Jessica went on to explain they were called netsuke. She said they were very old and rarely used for their original purpose, but were now mainly used as fastenings which had become extremely valuable and sought after.

'As a matter of fact, I know someone who has some netsuke, but I don't think she has any idea of their value.'

Lisa, who wasn't that interested in cultural matters, pricked her ears up at this news.

'Why, how much are they worth, then?'

'Well, I shouldn't be telling you all this, really, but I'm rather excited to have discovered them, to be honest. You won't believe it, but each one of these little beauties is worth a staggering quarter of a million pounds.'

Lisa sat up, suddenly very interested.

'Who is the lucky person who has them hidden away, Jess?'

'Again, this is top secret, but I know you haven't met Lady Soames, oh heck, there I go, you see I've let the cat out of the bag now,' said Jessica, holding her hand up to cover her mouth, as if that ought to have stopped her words from escaping, and she could somehow swallow them in again.

'Don't worry, Jess. As you said, I don't know the lady. I'm hardly going to meet her, so your secret is safe with me. Just out of interest, though, do you know how many she owns, have you actually seen them?' she tried to sound as casual as possible.

'Yes, you mustn't say anything, not even to Antony, Lisa. You can't let on, or I'd be out of a job. But I know I can trust you, and as you say, you're not likely to meet her.'

'How did you find out she had them?' Lisa tried again to glean the information she wanted.

'Last time I saw her she was wearing a very unusual summer coat, and I admired the fastenings, of which there were six, and she very casually said she had another six in her sewing basket. She'd been given them by an elderly aunt, who used to live in Japan.'

Lisa did a quick calculation in her head, realising there was three million pounds at stake here, and, keeping calm, changed the subject, but her palms were sweating, and her heart beating that little bit faster.

Her financial situation had never been on firm ground, living beyond her means was a way of life. She had spiralled into debt early on, and had no qualms about stealing or swindling those better off than her.

She needed to go home and work out a plan.

'OK, well I can see you're engrossed in your work, Jessica, so I'll love you and leave you,' said Lisa, nonchalantly, making her way towards the door.

Over the coming few weeks, she did some research of her own, and within that time, the unfortunate Jessica met with the fatal car crash.

At the funeral, Lisa was extremely attentive to poor Antony, who was devastated by his loss. She was cautious not to appear pushy or in any way more than a caring friend in his hour of need, but surreptitiously she observed his family, and the group of very close friends, amongst whom Lord and Lady Soames and their sons were a big part, she noted.

She bided her time, joined the am-dram society, gradually getting him back into leading the life he'd had before Jessica died, and encouraging him back to work in the local surgery, as a way of occupying his mind and coming to terms with his grief. She mopped up Antony's tears when occasion demanded, and was always careful not to overstep the mark, so he began to see her and lean on her as a strong and loyal friend.

She picked her moment with care, and when she finally seduced Antony, it was with subtlety and precision.

Therefore, it was no surprise to anyone when he invited

his new girlfriend to Starlington Hall on the annual barbecue weekend in August, and introduced her to his family and friends, who were delighted to see him moving on in his life.

Lord Duncan felt an air of familiarity about Lisa, but couldn't put his finger on it. She knew exactly who he was, but made sure to keep her distance, and was careful never to be alone with him. There was also a hint of recollection forthcoming from Antony's father, Richard Vickers, but from the dim and distant past, not the recent one.

She and Lady Soames did not hit it off.

Lisa had the feeling from the beginning that Philippa saw right through her. She was the one who asked the most awkward questions of her, putting Lisa on her guard, making her stumble over her words, and giving her the appearance of being far from bright. This condescending manner of Lady Soames, however, only served to make her all the more determined to get the better of the older, intelligent and extremely rich woman.

She had sent her unsavoury brother, Shane, to do a search of the house and grounds on several occasions, but he had gleaned no useful information. He had nearly got caught snooping by the gardener once as well. It was too close for comfort, so she realised she would need to gain entry to the house herself to be able to carry out the theft.

Annoyingly, the younger woman was thwarted at every turn in her search for the netsuke. When she'd attended the annual barbecue at Starlington Hall, she had first set about her task. Lady Soames' dressing room was situated off her bedroom, down two steps in the east wing. However, Philippa had made a big song and dance over how unhappy she was with this dressing room and told the entire party how she intended to move her dressing room to a new position. It would soon be located at the front of the house where there was plenty of light, she'd determined.

Lisa decided she'd have a better chance of discovering the netsuke, when they were installed in the more accessible space. She would need to be patient. There were only a few months to wait until the weekend of the shoot.

On the second visit to Starlington Hall, she learnt where the refurbished large sunny dressing room was situated, and was even happier to discover that she'd been accommodated very close by.

On the first day of the shoot, she stealthily crept along the corridor, having made sure every other guest was occupied. She made her way to the new dressing room and entered quietly. The room was untidy in the extreme, which shocked Lisa, imagining that Lady Soames, being of a practical nature, would have her clothes in a neat and orderly fashion. 'Of course,' she thought, '"the collection", which was being worked on by Gingham and Velvet.' Garments were hung on every conceivable hook, and not tucked away neatly. Lisa had a moment of panic, in which she racked her brain to try to remember when the fittings were to take place. She couldn't take a chance of being interrupted, so exited quickly, and descended the staircase to join the guests, who were now gathered in the drawing room, about to be served afternoon tea.

She sat with Paula and Nicky, feigning interest in their business, chatting about fashion and being overly friendly, which she knew had puzzled the two women, after her slightly frosty demeanour of their previous encounters, but she had pressed on regardless.

As casually as she could she asked the question she needed answering, to ascertain when the fittings were to take place.

'Not until tomorrow morning,' Nicky told her. 'When all the men have left to continue with the second day's shoot.'

Lisa continued to chat for a while longer, and then excused herself from the ghastly round of whist, which was taking place for the remaining guests, saying she wanted to spend some time in the library.

Most of the men were in their positions outside, but Richard Vickers was having trouble with his gun.

'I'm going to fetch my spare,' he quipped, leaving the terrace.

'I'm not sure it will make a whole lot of difference, old boy,' laughed Lord Duncan to his pal, as he made his way into the house.

The remaining men all joined him in the good-humoured ribbing, but Richard, without a backwards glance, continued on his objective.

When he reached the top of the stairs, and turned to walk along the corridor, he heard noises coming from Lady Soame' dressing room, and, being of a curious and playful nature, thought he'd surprise Philippa, just for the fun of it. He liked to tease her, and was probably one of the very few who could get away with it.

He entered the room quietly, wanting to give her a bit of a start for his own amusement, and got the shock of his life. Lisa was standing in the middle of the room wearing a pair of thin white gloves, and holding a pair of scissors, determinedly cutting off something from one of Philippa's coats, concentrating hard, and adding to a pile of others on a little table nearby. There was a detritus of sewing items strewn on the floor. She looked up, all of a sudden, and saw Richard's outraged face.

'What on earth are you doing, young lady?' asked a stunned Richard. 'Let me see what you've got there.'

Lisa panicked. 'Oh, it's nothing.'

Richard walked towards her, grappling with her now, as the odd fasteners and coat flew out of her grasp and onto the floor.

She picked all the netsuke up from the table and floor, holding them fast to her chest.

'Whatever you're doing, Lisa, I've caught you red-handed, you'd better come clean and tell me, or I'll have to get reinforcements.'

Lisa, though shaken, thought quickly, and pleaded to his better nature, so in a quiet, beseeching voice, she answered, 'I promise I'll tell you, in my room. Please, Richard, at least let me explain.'

'Well, be sharp about it. I'll give you five minutes, and the benefit of the doubt. I'll see you in your room.'

Lisa tidied away the sewing box things, where she'd found the first six netsuke, and then stuffed the coat back in the middle of the wardrobe. She scanned the room quickly, grabbed a photograph which showed off the netsuke as an afterthought, and crept along to her room, clutching the twelve precious items.

She took a deep breath, having hastily decided on her course of action.

When she entered her room, Richard was stood by the bed, trying to look stern.

She placed the netsuke and framed picture on her

bedside table, and peeled off her gloves.

She knew he could be pliable if she played her cards right. He'd chosen to forget all about the raucous parties back in the day, when, escaping from an unadventurous wife, and fuelled by drink and drugs, he'd enjoyed a lot of kinky and carefree sex with a host of young, highly expensive prostitutes, one of whom was right there in the room.

He needed to be reminded of what he'd been missing.

'You don't remember me, do you, Richard?'

'Of course I do. You're my son's girlfriend!'

'Ah, yes, Antony, your dear son. What do you think he and his mother would say if they knew what you got up to during your nights of passion? Do you still attend the parties, Richard? Where was it? I seem to recall it was always at a top-notch venue wasn't it? It was many years ago now. Wild times, full of drugs and kinky sex, plenty of frolics with young girls, and boys too, as I remember?'

Richard sat down on the edge of the bed, stunned and appalled, looking up with new eyes now, at this hard and bitter young woman. Out of the blue he saw, with clarity, the skinny young girl that she had once been.

'Oh my God, Lisa, that was you wasn't it?' he said, shakily. 'I always had a feeling there was something familiar about you, but the memory was vague and I could never put my finger on it.'

'Well, why would you remember a young, scrawny, scared creature, so drugged up she didn't know what she was doing, doing things to strangers, to men who hardly glanced at her face, just her naked body, writhing and complicit. Yes, familiar is the right word, Richard. I recognised you but kept my thoughts to myself, never wanting to rock the boat, give away your secrets. Oh yes I was discreet but I never forgot.'

'I'm so sorry, Lisa. I was younger and more audacious in those days, not thinking about the consequences of my actions,' Richard protested, gradually gaining his composure now. Changing tack, he went on. 'But young lady, that does not explain what you were doing in Lady P's dressing room.'

'None of that is any business of yours, and if you know what is good for you, you will forget you ever saw me in there, and then I'll forget all about the parties.'

Richard hesitated. 'I'll need to have a good think about all this, Lisa. I don't want my son involved in any more hurt, after what happened to Jessica. He's gone through enough.'

Lisa screwed up her eyes, calculatingly. 'Antony and Helen need never find out anything about your past. And who knows, Richard, we could resume our friendship if it would help you forget about this little incident. It may even be fun,' she said seductively.

'Now hang on a minute, we don't want to be hasty. This has come as a shock to the system. OK,' he said, coming to a snap decision. 'Let's both sleep on it, and resume this conversation tomorrow. I need to go down to join the others, they'll be wondering where I am. Nothing will be said for the time being, that I can promise you.'

'Good, that's more like it, Richard. Our little secret,' replied Lisa, touching her second finger to her mouth, and giving a cheeky wink. 'Go on now, be gone with you.'

He walked, with as much decorum as he could gather, rapidly collected the gun from his own bedroom, and headed downstairs.

'About time too,' called Lord Duncan when he saw his chum. 'We thought you'd given up the fight, old boy, let's see

235

if this new gun of yours makes any difference!'

Richard resumed his stance, but had an uncommonly bad aim for the rest of the day's shoot.

Whichever way Lisa looked at it, she knew that Richard would not be silenced for long. Yes, she could string him along, degrade herself by offering her body, and threaten him with exposure, knowing this would not only ruin his career but devastate his wife and son. But how could she be sure he wouldn't have a change of heart? No, she couldn't risk being found out. She would need to silence him forever.

She'd wondered about tampering with his gun, or his vehicle. That had worked on Jessica, there had been no suspicion about the faulty brakes on her VW golf in the aftermath of her accident. Why would there be?

Weed killer? Rat poison? There was bound to be some in one of the many outbuildings in the grounds. But even though she may find the poison, how would she administer it?

Port, a strong flavoured drink, the bottle of port laid out waiting for the men to drink after the banquet tonight?

But how to make sure he alone drank from the poisoned glass?

She would have to arrange an assignation with him, making sure she could provide the glass and the port.

So she set about making her plan. She was good at planning, was Lisa.

Darn that housekeeper and gardener, and then the dratted dressmaker. She knew they'd been curious as to why she'd been in the greenhouse, and had fleetingly been grateful to her granny Apple for the information she'd imparted to Lisa about her obsession with orchids. She'd thought them a "posh" plant. Lisa realised now it was her granny Apple's influence, harping on about those bloody orchids that had started her off, daring to dream of a better life, and having ideas above her station. Yes, granny Apple had a lot to answer for.

During the banquet, Lisa kept her eye on Richard, who was very subdued, surreptitiously glancing in her direction when he dared. She smiled over at him several times, but he turned away before she could meet his eyes.

When the meal was finished, the men were to stay behind to start on the port in earnest. Cheese and port had been served to the ladies initially, but more bottles appeared on the table, and, having caught Richard's eye at last, Lisa had indicated with force that she wanted to see him outside.

Everyone had consumed a vast amount of alcohol, and all of the guests were milling about in the vestibule, searching for a bathroom or cloakroom, so in the confusion which followed, Richard, anxious now to speak with Lisa, was able to slip away unnoticed.

He quickly saw her sat at a table on the far side of the terrace which was out of sight, completely in the dark.

'Hello, Richard, do come and join me.' She indicated for him to be seated.

She had managed to secure half a bottle of port in a small decanter, and had already poured out a glass for each of them.

'Cheers, Richard,' she said, handing him a glass.

She was easily able to disguise the fact that she was not drinking. He gulped down several large mouthfuls, in his anxiety and agitation.

'Look, I can't be out here long, Lisa, what was so urgent

that it couldn't wait until tomorrow?'

'Nothing in particular, Richard, I just wanted you to know I won't be spilling the beans, you looked so ill at ease during the meal, I just wanted to reassure you.'

'Of course not, nor me, but I must be going now, I'll be missed,' he gulped down the remains of the port, got up and departed, brushing his hand over her arm on the way.

Lisa waited until he was inside, and then set about burying the evidence in the deep hole she'd prepared in the early evening darkness. She'd hidden the fatal bottle of poison that she'd mixed with the port beforehand, in the undergrowth nearby. Now she dropped in the glasses and small decanter and filled the hole with plenty of earth. Her plan had succeeded, and so, with a satisfied smirk, she went inside to join the ladies in the drawing room, having deftly slipped into the nearest cloakroom on the way to clean up and compose herself.

She hadn't realised in her haste that a loosened gemstone had dropped easily out of its loose setting from her beloved pendant, as she'd bent over, plummeting into the hole, alongside the vital evidence.

Looking around, now, at the sea of faces, all aghast, she bowed her head. Out of the corner of her eye she saw the look of devastation on the face of Antony. That is the one regret she had felt in this whole sorry business, and one of the reasons she'd agreed to accompany him today. The other thing she needed to do was to remove the summer coat she'd left behind by mistake in Lady P's wardrobe. It was, she realised now, her fatal mistake. She was led out of the room by the policeman. On walking past her ex-boyfriend, she hesitated, touching his hand briefly and meeting his eyes. She said in a strained voice, 'I'm so sorry Anton.'

Antony, as if touched by a scorpion, pulled his hand away in disgust and looked the other way.

The room was silent.

CHAPTER TWENTY-THREE

Paula and Nicky were persuaded to stay an extra night in Hampshire, by their hosts because when they had finally bid farewell to the stunned guests, and the remaining ones were flopped in front of the fire, exhausted, it was much later than anticipated.

Vivienne, having cleared away the debris from the buffet, had enough food left over to lay on a smaller spread, along with a few tasty additions, for the residual visitors.

So, in addition to the four family members, the remaining faction found themselves sitting down to eat in the family dining room, at a fairly late hour.

The discourse inevitably focused on the events of the day.

Isobel did not hold back in her questioning of the two girls, neither did she have a filter when it came to projecting her opinions.

'All these unpalatable truths we learned about Daddy had nothing to do with the outcome in the end. We needn't have been subjected to the cruel scrutiny of his life. It seems so unfair to have put us all through it.'

'Isobel, you can't say that,' admonished Lord Duncan. 'The police had to look for a motive. They had to start somewhere, and who could have guessed at the unexpected result, or indeed have believed that young lady capable of such an act?'

'She nearly got away with it too,' put in Nicky. 'I don't understand why she continued to wear the pendant, having lost one of the rubies... it must have been a favourite. I suppose she intended to replace the stone at some point.'

'Yes. It had belonged to her granny. The one good piece of jewellery she had ever owned,' said Antony, quietly.

The conversation ground to a halt with this revelation, everyone feeling ill at ease and tongue-tied.

'I think I'll have an early night, if no one minds,' continued Antony, rising from his chair and heading towards the door.

'Goodnight, son, and God bless,' said Helen in a sad voice. Isobel was about to retort, but Helen put her hand over Isobel's mouth. 'No,' she said in a dramatic fashion.

It wasn't long before everyone started to make an excuse to retire for the night, so there were just five people remaining, now sat in the back snug. Each was nursing a brandy glass, swirling the amber liquid, in between sipping and feeling the warmth trickle through their bodies, and staring, mesmerisingly at the flames of the open fire.

At an earlier time, the Scotland Yard detective had briefly outlined the salient points of the murder enquiry to the shocked spectators.

Back in the moment, in the back snug, The Twizzler said, 'You should be very proud of yourselves, ladies.'

'Oh, thanks,' said Nicky and Paula in unison, emerging from their reverie.

'How on earth did you link the, what are they called, those Japanese things?' asked Toby.

'Netsuke,' replied Paula. 'They're worth a fortune. Your

mother had no idea of their value. When I checked on the Internet, it all became so obvious and everything seemed to slot into place. We had no idea at that stage whom the guilty party was. We just felt it all had to be linked.'

'Quick thinking, that's what it was. You were amazing. No one else would have put two and two together,' said Will.

'When I spotted the gap in the pendant which Lisa was wearing, and pointed it out to Paula, we both realised the significance. I still can't quite believe it. Lisa. Who would have thought it? I feel so hopelessly sad for Anton,' said Nicky, echoing the thoughts of everyone in the room.

'I can't begin to imagine what he's going through,' agreed Paula.

'Most men would have gone under after everything he's had to endure. I'm going to suggest a complete change of scene. In fact, I may hop on a plane with him. We could travel to the Far East.'

'Good idea, bro. Some of your Eastern teachings could be just the thing for him right now,' said Toby, wisely. 'Yes, it's a splendid idea.'

'I'm warming to this by the minute. How about it, ladies, do you fancy a trip? You could join us,' said Will, unexpectedly.

'We'll have to see about that, Will,' laughed Paula. 'It's all a bit sudden!'

'I know that's because I've only just cooked up the idea, but now that I have, I rather like the sound of it!'

'Hmmm,' Nicky pondered, thinking out loud.   'It could be in the new year. Some winter sun… halcyon days… I must say it does sound tempting…'

The Twizzler was sitting in his favourite chair, stroking his moustache, finding it hard to keep awake. He kept drifting away to another place. He'd always known there was something familiar about Lisa, and today, the penny finally dropped... After the disclosure, she'd switched between portraying herself as a pathetic creature to a chillingly calculating one. It was that single cruel look to the eyes that had given the game away. He knew he'd be steering clear of the infamous burlesque club from now on. Instead of feeling saddened or hurt, he found his overriding emotion was one of relief. He could finally put a stop to that period of his life, which he was certain he'd never want to revisit. Glancing over at the vibrant young people in front of the cosy fire, all of a sudden he felt older, yet strangely contented.

Christmas gifts, fairy lights, tinsel, plum puddings and rich game pie. These were some of the things that Nicky and Paula were both busy with over the next few weeks.

There was quite a tumult in the media with regard to the solving of the murder in Hampshire of Richard Vickers. Lisa Moore and her brother, Shane, (the Lone Walker), who looked, from his photograph, to be woven of a shady cloth, were being held in custody awaiting trial. As with any other sensational news, it held the front page and news headlines for a few days and then became relegated to the recycling pile.

Both girls decorated their respective homes with zest and creativity, as well as their beloved barn.

Paula still thought about her ex-lover every day, but his image was starting to fade a little, and her broken heart was slowly mending.

Preparations were under way for the big Christmas Eve party, taking place at the barn, to welcome Poppy home from her travels.

On a late December day, two separate cars sped down the motorway, both heading in the same direction, their destination being, in fact, the very same.

Freddy had managed to wheedle his way into the driving seat; somehow persuading Nicky it was a spiffing idea for him to be the chauffeur. Paula was rather put out to start with, then decided to drop it, knowing how much pleasure he'd derive from seeing his Goddaughter return to the fold.

When Nicky, Leonard, Paula and Freddy stood, ahead of time awaiting the arrival of Poppy's flight, Paula received a tap on her shoulder and turned to see her daughter, Tegan. She was dressed from head to toe in bright emerald green, complete with tinkle belled hat and frizzy black wig. She'd either secured a cut price elf's outfit, or stolen someone's uniform from an Irish themed pub. Each time she moved her head, the bells jingled frantically, and they all burst into spontaneous laughter, much to the amusement of the waiting crowd.

'Only you,' said Paula, hugging her close.

'Do you think there's been a delay?' asked Leonard, anxiously, when the laughter died down.

'No, I just think we're too early, Dad. It won't be long now,' replied Nicky.

And then, suddenly, there she was.

A golden haired, bronzed, slim and attractive young lady, dressed in a bright blue top, navy blue fisherman's pants and flip-flops was coming into view. Her hair was longer, wavier